THIRD CRIME'S THE CHARM

A CHARM ISLAND MYSTERY
BOOK 2

CASEY GRIFFIN

CHARMING FROG
PUBLISHING

ISBN: 978-1-990470-34-9

First Paperback Edition: April 2025

Published by Charming Frog Publishing

www.CharmingFrogPublishing.com

LET CASEY HAUNT YOUR INBOX

Casey Griffin's newsletter followers get access to exclusive content, fun gifts, and random shenanigans (because who doesn't love those?). You'll also get *Dead Ringer*, a FREE NOVELLA that takes place after this book!

Sign up at
CASEYGRIFFIN.COM

CHAPTER ONE

Hangers scraped across rods as I browsed for clothes with my BFF Alice, a cat, and my fiancé's ghost—though whether I should still call Nolan my fiancé was a sensitive subject. For all my fears of returning home to Charm Island, it had been no sweat to slip back into normal life. Okay, shopping with a cat was a first for me. Shopping with a ghost, however, was not. Lucky me.

Alice and I flicked through new and secondhand designs, seeking the perfect uniform for her baking business, an idea I'd lovingly nudged her into—well, more like shoved. After being MIA for five years, I'd vowed to make it up to my loved ones. First on the list: help Alice fulfill all her baking dreams.

She held up a plain blouse for me to see. "Hey, Violet. What about this one?"

I pursed my lips. It did nothing for her porcelain skin or dark brown hair. She needed something that popped. "It doesn't say you're selling delicious baked goods. More like you're selling insurance." I took it from her and faced it toward the little black cat lounging on a pile of folded angora sweaters. "What do you think, Zelda?"

She yawned and flicked her tail before readjusting herself

to display her backside. If the owner of the consignment store took offense at Zelda's opinion, she kept it to herself. Nor did she seem to mind the feline hanging around. Then again, she had three of her own cats lolling in scarf baskets and knocking hats off shelves. I assumed they were the inspiration for the shop's name: Mew to You. It meant you had to defur anything you purchased, but it made for a happier shopping experience.

When I moved to the next rack, I found Nolan's ethereal form hanging out in the middle of it. Since the dim lighting made him appear almost solid, it looked like he wore the top he stood behind. It was a lacy red number with a plunging neckline.

He flicked his caramel-colored hair dramatically. "How do I look?"

A surprised snort escaped me, loud in the quiet store. Startled, an orange tabby cat wailed and leaped off a nearby shoe display, knocking over a pair of suede stilettos. I snatched the top off the rack before Nolan sent me into a fit of giggles. In a small town, one could only talk to their cat and laugh to themselves so much before people started to wonder.

Alice gaped at the shirt. "I don't think that's the right look either. It says I'm selling more than baked goods, if you know what I mean."

I replaced the racy top. "You're right. I'm not sure what I was thinking." I flashed Nolan a warning look that told him to knock it off.

Stepping out of the rack, he straightened the three-piece suit he'd died in, a step up from the lacy red shirt. While he appeared dashing 24/7, it made me hope that if I ever wound up as a ghost, it would be in my loungewear.

He strolled over to another shirt and presented it with a grand sweep of his hand. "Might I interest you in the new arrivals section?"

Turning to eye the shirt, I pressed my lips together,

prepared for his usual silliness. But actually, his pick wasn't a bad choice.

I showed it to Alice. "What about this one? The black button-up style says you're a serious professional, while the pink polka dots and puffy sleeves say 'seriously fun!' Plus there are several of them, so you can buy a few to have backups."

Her hazel eyes lit up. "It would match my branding perfectly."

"Branding?" I arched a quizzical eyebrow.

"I've been studying marketing tips online. Like you said, I'm a serious professional now. I've got business cards and everything. I'm still working on my website, though, so it's not available to the public."

She pulled out her phone and brought up a web page. *Batch of the Day* scrolled across the top in a cheerful font, accompanied by a cupcake on the end of a fishing line, fitting right in with the town's marine-related theme. It rested against a black header with, yup, bubblegum-pink polka dots.

"It looks great," I gushed. "I can't believe how much you've accomplished with your busy schedule. If you ever need me to take anything off your plate, you only have to ask."

She tucked her phone away. "I've got it covered. You have enough to worry about, what with helping your dad at the jewelry shop and settling back in. I mean, this is the first time you've returned since… you know."

Since my fiancé's car veered off a cliff, taking his life, nearly ending mine, and leaving me with the ability to communicate with ghosts? Yeah, I did know, but I shrugged it off, especially because my friend wasn't aware of the last one. "I'm fine. Everything's fine. Besides, it's not like I have anything else going on."

Nolan cleared his throat. "No. Nothing at all. Certainly not solving my murder."

I suppressed a wince as guilt stabbed me in the heart. I'd

get to Nolan's case. Soon. I just had a lot to do for my more-alive loved ones since time was literally still ticking for them.

Alice clicked her tongue. "You've already done so much for me. In fact, I never would have started Batch of the Day if not for your encouragement."

"If not for my arm-twisting, you mean." I ducked my head, sorry but also not sorry.

"Much-appreciated arm-twisting." She turned her attention back to the polka dot shirt and flipped over the price tag. "Ouch. On second thought, I'll pass. I've already spent too much setting up the business. I'll wear something I have in my closet for now."

She returned it to the rack, but I didn't miss how she cast one more longing look over her shoulder before we exited the shop.

Our lunch breaks nearly over, Alice and I headed for Spread the Word, where she worked full time as the only baker on staff. I couldn't tell if Nolan was with us, since the midday sun was out in full force, and light altered my ability to see spirits clearly. However, I didn't doubt he was following me. He did that a lot, whether I wanted him to or not.

As we walked along the boardwalk that connected the entire downtown core, Zelda accompanied us, darting between our legs. At the next intersection, she veered toward the marina.

"Tired of shopping already?" I called after her.

She fixed me with a bored look. *I have better things to do.* Since she could control who "heard" her telepathy, to anyone else, it would have sounded something like "Meow."

"We both know all you're going to do is lie around and lick yourself."

As I said, better things. She skittered off, tail held high.

Alice watched me, amusement dancing in her eyes. "I don't know what's stranger. That you talk to a cat so often or how she actually seems to understand you."

I forced a laugh. *Nothing to see here, folks. Just an ordinary pet.*

In reality, Zelda was a familiar—not my familiar, which she loved to rub in my face. She was Nolan's, since he'd been a witch in life. Or a warlock, I supposed. I hadn't learned about all that stuff yet, much to the eternal frustration of Helen, my mentor. Unfortunately, since she was my next-door neighbor, I couldn't avoid my powers forever. As much as I wanted to.

We rounded the corner onto Beluga Boulevard, and a woman's raised voice carried through the air. I searched for the source and recognized the owner of I Knead Bread right away. Even from behind, Ingrid was easy to spot by her red hair that could only be found in a box. Also, the floury apron still tied around her waist was a dead giveaway.

Fists on her hips, she stood behind a delivery truck, shouting through the open back door. "Where are they? Huh? What did you do with my supplies?" Her voice had a crumbly texture to it, like the shortbread she sold during the holidays.

When we got closer, I peered inside the truck. An exasperated man stacked boxes onto a dolly, muttering something under his breath. He flicked aside strands of hair that had fallen out of his bun and wheeled his delivery down the metal ramp.

"I told you, lady. They're not in my truck. I don't know what you want me to do." To end the conversation, he steered his dolly toward the coffee shop, Full of Beans.

She planted herself in his path and thrust out her arms in a terrible impression of a starfish. "I know he has them. Admit it. How much did he pay you?"

Alice and I slowed to watch the confrontation—there wasn't much to do in Hope, so we found our entertainment where we could. As the delivery guy darted around her, I had to leap out of the way before he ran over my foot.

Ingrid stomped after him as if testing the boardwalk's structural integrity. She clipped me on the shoulder as she passed. I stared after her in disbelief until the shop's door closed, muffling her complaints.

Alice faced me with wide eyes. "What was that about?"

"I'm not sure." Brushing it off as Ingrid being her usual antagonistic self, I contemplated the delivery vehicle. "What about a food truck?"

"We just ate. You can't be hungry again."

"No. Okay, yes. I was planning to grab some muffins from the bakery." I waved it off. "What I mean is you should buy a food truck for your business. It might be cheaper than renting a storefront. What do you think?"

She shook her head at me and continued down the boardwalk. "I think you're more obsessed with my business than I am. And I'm not ready for that. Besides, I was only going to specialize in cakes. That way, I'd take orders in advance, and I won't be in direct competition with Spread the Word."

"Really?" I stared at her. "Don't get me wrong. Your cakes are works of art, but you can do so much more than that. Your cookies are swoonworthy, and your macarons are…" I made an unintelligible noise as I reminisced about her last batch: salted brown sugar and caramel. "Who cares if you're competing with the bakery? Isn't that the point?"

Alice slowed as we approached her workplace, keeping her voice hushed. "Well, I do still bake for Roman."

"Wait…" I wedged myself between her and the door. "You still haven't told him about your new business, have you?"

She drew me aside like we were talking about something scandalous, not baked goods. "I was waiting for the right moment. I just know what he's like, and I'm afraid he'll overreact."

"Who cares what that man thinks?" I crossed my arms. "He treats you like garbage while he lines his overstuffed pockets with your talent. You are the best baker on Charm Island. No, in the world. It's time you have your cake and eat it too."

She groaned and rolled her eyes.

I frowned. Was I overstepping or pushing too hard again? "Isn't that what you want?"

She giggled. "I do. I was groaning at your joke. And I know you're right, but I need more time."

Alice worried so much about helping everyone else that sometimes she put herself last, even after a terrible boss like Roman. But I didn't push the issue. She'd worked at the bakery since high school. It was her second home, almost literally since she spent so much time there. Who was I to come in after a five-year absence and yank her out of her comfort zone? Once she had her business up and running, she'd see she was better off. Until then, maintaining a safe, stable job might be exactly what she needed.

As Alice opened the door to the bakery, footsteps thundered down the boardwalk behind us.

"Move it or lose it," ordered a harsh voice.

We leaped aside as Ingrid blew past us and through the open door. She'd barely stepped inside before she started yelling.

"Roman, you lowlife! You rotten, cheating thief! You're a dead man!"

Okay. Maybe Spread the Word wasn't so safe after all.

CHAPTER TWO

Alice and I followed the trail of Ingrid's vicious insults into the bakery, squeezing past a line of people that snaked from the counter to the door. Lucy Litton, a reporter for *The Siren*, stood near the back. She scowled at me as though I were cutting in front of her at a popular club. I pointed to Alice in an I'm-with-the-band gesture and stood off to the side. While I'd wait until the crowd cleared to buy my muffins, I wanted a front-row seat for whatever was about to go down.

The interior was dim despite the sunny day. The awning above the front window blocked the afternoon rays, and all the lights were off. For a moment, I blamed Charm Island's quaint habit of rolling blackouts. However, the display cases still glowed, highlighting a colorful array of treats. The owner must have relished cutting corners on bills just as much as he did on employee wages.

Thanks to the mood lighting, I could see Nolan again. He joined the lineup as if waiting to buy some goodies. I wondered if he was trying to lighten the mood or if he'd forgotten why he was there. Sometimes, it seemed he did things out of human habit, like when he covered his mouth to sneeze. And come to think of it, why would a ghost need to sneeze?

Alice hurried past a fuming Ingrid and rounded the counter, where her boss, Roman, was working for once. The robust sixty-year-old was tall, with muscles that said he could still win a bar fight at Killer Ale. As he hunched over the cash register, pecking the buttons uncertainly, he resembled a gorilla attempting to thread a needle.

Ingrid tapped the toe of her sneaker on the black-and-white tile floor. He completely ignored her as he finished helping a customer. It only aggravated the bread maker more, her foot beating faster in an aggressive tap dance.

Finally, she rapped on the display case to get his attention. "I haven't got all day, Roman. You've got some nerve. Where is it?"

He stared at her as a bull would a fly. "Where is what? My nerve?"

"You know what. My supply shipment. I was supposed to receive it this morning, like everyone else on the island. Only it never showed up. I spoke with the delivery guy, and he says it's not on the truck, but I bet you received yours."

"I did," Roman said, his tone mocking. "Thank you very much for your concern."

She pointed a flour-caked finger at him. "How much did you pay him to get your hands on my goods?"

He leveled her with a flat look. "I can assure you I want nothing to do with your goods. That was twenty years ago. Get over it."

A few chuckles rose from the waiting patrons, but when Ingrid wheeled on them, her round cheeks flushing, the snickers died. People quickly averted their gazes, suddenly engrossed in their phones. Lucy held hers up, likely recording the interaction, and by the way she licked her lips, the blond craved a tasty story more than a cookie.

Ingrid smoothed the front of her apron before turning back to Roman. "You know perfectly well what I mean."

Laying his palms on the countertop, he leaned closer. "If

you want to know where your stuff is, take it up with your supplier."

Alice finished washing her hands and donned an apron. Quiet as a mouse, she grabbed a pair of tongs and squeezed beside him.

Roman shifted his glare to her. "Where have you been?" Not giving her a chance to answer, he snatched the tongs from her. "Take over the till. I can't get it to work. There's something wrong with it."

Ingrid leaned closer to me and stage-whispered so the whole place could hear. "More like there's something wrong with the operator."

Giving her a half-hearted smile, I took a step back and joined a woman waiting for her order in the dark corner. While I was content to stay and watch the show, I didn't want to take part. Alice wasn't wrong about Roman's tendency to overreact. If I got lumped in with Ingrid, the man might ban me from his establishment along with her. Then where would I buy my carrot ginger muffins?

Alice switched places with Roman and rang the customer through in under fifteen seconds. "What happened to Caitlin? Did she go home sick?"

"She quit on me. Can you believe it? Said working here isn't worth minimum wage." He closed his eyes in exasperation. "Young people these days."

Ingrid snorted. "What? Roman Fedoro can't handle a woman's rejection?"

Apparently, a jab at his prowess with the opposite sex was the way to push his buttons. He held up palms the size of bear claws—the baked kind, not the furry kind. "It wasn't my fault. Is it illegal to compliment a woman these days?"

I scoffed. That depended on the "compliment."

"Can't win 'em all. Can you, Roman?" Ingrid said then raised her voice to yell at an older man near the back of the line. "Ain't that right, Milton?!"

I thought she was seeking support from others in the room. However, when the man named Milton lowered the brim of his hat as though he hoped it would eat him whole, there seemed to be more to the comment. Ingrid cackled like they were sharing a joke, but the flush across his dark cheeks said he didn't appreciate her particular brand of humor.

Roman planted a meaty fist on his hip. "Was there something else you wanted, Ingrid? Or did you just want to blame me for your inability to run a business? Because if you're quite done, I have a prosperous bakery to run." He gestured to the waiting customers. "Not that you'd know what that looks like."

Her mouth opened and closed until she resembled a shocked fish out of water, lips quivering with all the insults fighting to be first out.

Lucy's eyebrows shot up, and some of the other patrons shifted, probably rethinking their need for carbs. Nolan appeared uncomfortable, too, which was odd, considering no one else but me could see him.

I eyed the woman hiding in the darkened corner with me. She tugged on the salt-and-pepper braid that hung to her waist, looking desperate for her order so she could get out of there. When she met my gaze, she did a double take like she recognized me.

Though her face didn't ring a bell, she might have seen me around in the past. There weren't many people on the island with natural red hair like mine, so I was hard to miss. I gave her a smile, and her lip twitched before she refocused on the dramatic scene.

When Ingrid couldn't settle on a scathing response, Roman waved up the next person in line. "How can I help you?"

A willowy woman in a pencil skirt sashayed to the glass case and held out a crisp, white paper. "I believe I am the one who can help you." Her melodic voice lilted with a heavy and seductive French accent. While she could have easily passed for thirty, her timeless beauty might have landed her around ten years older than that.

Roman took the paper and read. "Colette Roche… This is a résumé?"

"I am applying for a position as head baker. I trained at the La Pâtisserie Dorée in Paris and studied under the tutelage of the renowned pastry chef Pierre Dubois."

He blinked at her as if trying to translate what she'd said, even though she'd spoken perfect English. "But can you bake?"

Her long eyelashes fluttered like she was suppressing an eye roll. "*Oui*. I can bake."

"Well, I don't need another baker. So unless you operate a till, I've got no work for you."

As he handed back the résumé, she hesitated before taking it. Her sharp eyebrows arched as if she wasn't used to hearing no.

Ingrid cut in. "I'd take her on if I were you, Roman. You go through bakers like you go through women. You've never treated your staff right, and now, even kind Alice has had enough of you."

He cocked his head. "What do you mean?"

A loud clatter pierced the air as Alice dropped a customer's change on the counter. With shaking hands, she scrambled to gather it while trying to signal Ingrid to stop.

Oblivious, the bread baker raised her nose in the air, pleased as her famous cherry pie. "She's obviously had enough abuse from you. I saw the website for her new business this morning. People only come to this dump for Alice's baking, and now, you're going to lose her along with all your customers."

Roman's face reddened. The plastic tongs in his large hand snapped, breaking into several pieces. The color drained from Alice's cheeks until it looked like she'd face-dived into a pile of flour. As the tension skyrocketed, three customers mumbled excuses and left. Not Lucy, obviously.

My stomach shriveled, and I fumbled in my pocket for my phone. I typed in Batch of the Day's website address. A few seconds later, my screen filled with pink polka dots. Alice's not-yet-public website—or so she'd thought. She must have made it accessible without meaning to.

Ingrid aimed a wink at Alice, as though they were on the same team. When she caught sight of my friend's expression, her smug attitude faltered.

She glanced from Roman to Alice and back again. "But… surely, you knew about it. You can't take advantage of your employees and expect them to stick around."

He huffed a breath through his flared nostrils, but his tone remained eerily calm. "Oh, indeed. I wouldn't want anyone to stick around if they're not happy in my employment."

Alice fidgeted with her apron. "I haven't even opened for business yet. It's only in the beginning stages. I was going to tell you—"

"When?!" he bellowed, causing everyone remaining in the store to jump. "After you stole my customers out from under me?"

"No," she squeaked. "I'm just going to bake cakes, so I wouldn't compete with you at all."

"After everything I've done for you over the years." He pressed a thick hand to his chest. "I've provided you with a steady job and good pay."

Unable to stand by any longer, I stomped to the counter. "And she works hard in return, but you take advantage of her. You have her coming in twice a day, seven days a week, and she sees nothing for the overtime since you pay her a 'salary.'" I made air quotes with my fingers.

"It's true." Alice's head bobbed. "I've hardly had a real day off in months."

He barked a laugh. "That's the thanks I get for giving you a raise?"

Ingrid wagged a finger. "Don't you gaslight her. This is your own doing. Same old Roman. You never change!"

Alice yanked off her apron and threw it at his chest. "She's right. You push everyone around and convince them to thank you for it. You're a bully who can't make a ready-to-bake cookie to save your life. You don't deserve my baking or the customers who eat it, and I'll happily take them from you."

I stared at my normally soft-spoken friend in shock. "Bravo."

"You're welcome to try, but I have a pastry chef from Paris now." Roman held out a hand to the French woman who'd been watching the interaction with indifference. "Let me see that résumé again. Turns out I do have an opening for a baker." His too-white teeth flashed. "And I think we'll add cake to the menu."

Alice grabbed her purse and stormed out from behind the counter. Her red-rimmed eyes glistened with unshed tears, but she held her delicate chin high. I linked my arm through hers in solidarity, and we marched for the exit.

As we passed through the door, Roman's voice carried out after us. "In case it isn't clear, Alice, you're fired!"

CHAPTER THREE

Alice and I charged out of the bakery, hurrying to put distance between us and her boss… er, her ex-boss. That didn't stop him from continuing his rant, though. His bellowing followed us down the boardwalk.

"And another thing—"

Thankfully, the bakery door shut, cutting him off.

Arm in arm, we strode to the end of the block. However, by the time we got there, Alice was shaking. I led her to a wrought iron bench in front of the liquor store, I Don't Give a Sip, which was convenient since she looked like she needed a drink.

I laid a hand on her shoulder. "It's going to be okay."

With a dazed expression, she nodded. "You're right. Roman just needs time to cool off. And we don't even know if this French woman can bake." She gripped my forearms. "He might still give me my job back, right?"

"Sure," I lied to ease her tortured expression. "Or you could fall back on your savings and focus on Batch of the Day. I'll help you find so many gigs that you'll be baking 24/7. You'll see."

"Maybe." Alice dashed away a tear and stood. "I've got to make a few phone calls. I'll talk to you later."

"But—"

"I'm fine, Vi. Really."

I didn't believe that for a second.

"Why don't you hang out with me this afternoon?" I asked. "Use the shop's phone to make your calls. We'll keep each other company, and you can share worst-boss-ever stories about Roman."

She laughed weakly. "There's not enough time in the day to share all of them. But I should really go. I'll be okay. I promise."

It was clear my friend was devastated, and while I knew how much she cared about her job, there was more than sadness in her expression. Panic flickered in her eyes. What wasn't she telling me?

Although I wanted to push her for more, it was obvious she wanted to be alone. "Okay. I'll call you later. I can bring over a bottle of wine tonight, and we'll watch a rom-com."

Her lips curled into something that resembled a smile. "Sounds good."

As she left for home, the part I'd played in her unemployment weighed on me. My encouragement surrounding her new business—okay, pushiness—had started a chain reaction that imploded her life. I wanted to chase after her and do something, even if it was only to cheer her up. However, I'd already been gone from the store too long, and my dad would want a break soon. He'd been needing a lot of those as of late. So I turned for the promenade.

I'd only passed a few shops before a voice, too close to my ear, asked, "Where are you going?"

Yelping, I whipped around to search for the source. At first, I saw nothing, then the air in front of me shifted like heat ripples rising from hot pavement. It was Nolan.

I breathed a sigh of relief until I spotted a woman eyeing me warily. Thinking fast, I swatted at the air. "It was a bee. I'm allergic."

Carrying on down the boardwalk, I brought my phone to my ear so I could talk to Nolan without drawing attention. "I'm going to work. Stop talking to me in public."

A disembodied chuckle drifted through the air. "No one said you had to talk back."

"What happened to your promise to give me space? Ever since I got back, you've been my shadow."

He huffed. "What happened to your promise to solve my murder and help me move on?"

I wanted to ask if he'd continue to haunt me until I did so, but I bit my tongue. The term "haunt" was harsh. He simply hung around. A lot.

"Don't worry," I said. "I'm working on it, but it's not like you've given me much to go on."

"I told you. Whenever I try to recall anything related to the accident, I come up… blank."

I remembered how Wyatt Thorn, the only spirit I'd ever helped move on, had seemed fuzzy on the details of his death too. It might have been a ghost thing. I supposed it was a blessing for the deceased, but it was inconvenient when one was trying to solve their murder. There was one hot tip I'd received, though: Nolan's father had influenced the sheriff to drop the case. However, it wasn't as if I could approach the mayor and ask, "Don't you care that your son was murdered? Don't you want answers? Justice?" So until I had more to back up my suspicions, I wouldn't share them with Nolan.

I shook it off. "It doesn't matter. I'll figure it out on my own. I promise. But digging up a cold-case murder everyone believes is an accident is going to take time."

We reached the end of Beluga Boulevard, and the wooden planks stretched out to form the promenade that overlooked the marina. I cut across it, passing the huge gazebo in the center on my way to the jewelry shop.

The air glimmered in front of me as Nolan blocked my path. "I'll help you investigate. I'd be the Watson to your Sherlock."

While I could have walked right through him, I didn't enjoy the chill it caused, especially not on such a cool spring day when all I had on was a light jacket. Plus the idea creeped me out.

"I don't need help," I said, trying to go around him.

He blocked me again. "But my ability to walk through walls and eavesdrop unseen might come in handy. And once Helen helps you explore your powers, you'll have a few tricks up your sleeve too. We'll be unstoppable."

Clutching my jacket tighter around me, I plowed through him. "This isn't the best time for Witchcraft 101. I've gotten by for twenty-seven years without ghosts or powers, and I will continue to do so. I just need time. And space."

Part of me knew his plan made sense. After all, it wasn't like I'd solved Wyatt's murder all by myself; technically, his ghost had helped. But I wasn't ready to begin my witchy lessons with Helen. Moving back home had been a big enough step. *One thing at a time.* Besides, being a human was all I knew how to be, and I was good at it—mostly.

I pocketed my phone and gripped the ring on my finger. Though it felt strange to wear the diamond eternity band Nolan had picked out for our ill-fated wedding day, jewelry acted as a conduit for my power. Since the piece had held such importance to Nolan in life, it allowed me to hear him in the afterlife. Not that it was always a good thing. "Now, don't make me take this off."

"All right. All right. I can take a hint." His voice faded away as he left to do whatever ghosts did when they weren't bugging me.

A weight settled in the pit of my stomach. I knew I wasn't being fair. Zelda and I were the only ones he could talk to—aside from the occasional other ghost in town, and they weren't exactly the life of the party. But every time I saw him, every time I spoke with him, it reminded me of the night I'd lost him and my powers emerged. The night I'd survived the "accident" and he didn't.

Of all the abilities I could have had, why ghosts? I mean, what good were they except to torture me? To remind me of my loss, of everyone's loss, something I couldn't undo no matter how much I wanted to.

On my way past the marina, I looked down to scan the moored boats, seeking one in particular: the *Crescent*. It was a navy blue-and-white sailboat that belonged to Max Nicolas, Nolan's best friend and my… I wasn't sure what anymore. We weren't on the best of terms since, you know, I'd ghosted him for five years only to return and accuse him of murder. Sadly, his boat-slash-house was still missing, as it had been for a couple of weeks. It looked like we wouldn't be working out our issues any time soon.

Through the gossip circuit, I'd heard he'd landed a carpentry job at the new resort under construction on the west side of the island. It was a pretty big deal, and while I was happy he'd secured the coveted gig, the way we'd left things hung over me.

I sighed and headed for the shop at the end of the promenade. Charming Treasures. The custom jewelry store had been in our family for multiple generations since Hope City was first established. Though, the town's name was a bit misleading; it hadn't been a bustling metropolis back then, and it certainly wasn't now.

My latest creations sparkled behind the multipaned bay windows on either side of the door. After being abroad, it felt so good to create again. It was as though I'd been stockpiling inspiration during my European travels, and now, it was exploding out of me.

When I heaved open the heavy wooden door, the bell above it tinkled. I slipped through the narrow shop lined with the original wood shelves and displays. Things were almost back to normal, the way they'd been since I could crawl through the place. Only a few signs of the recent break-in remained, like the antique cases near the front waiting for a custom glass order.

Dad popped his balding head out of the back room. "Oh, you're here. Are you okay on your own if I take off for a few hours?"

I didn't miss how he massaged his casted arm, the one that had been busted during the robbery. Dad pushed himself harder than he should, but he rarely complained, so I knew he must be hurting.

I decided the news about Alice could wait until later and shooed him away. "Why don't you take the rest of the day off? Things have been slow, so I can watch the front. I'll see you back at home."

"I think I will," he said, confirming my worries. Halfway out the door, he paused. "Keep an eye out for Zelda. She was in here earlier, but I haven't seen her in a while. The way she comes and goes, you'd think she walks through walls."

My eyebrows rose, but I didn't confirm or deny it. I suspected the feline possessed more skills than the ability to communicate telepathically, but I wasn't about to tell him that. For one thing, he might change his mind about taking in the "stray." For another, it would push him over the edge with the whole magic thing.

He'd come a long way in accepting I was a witch, something he'd kept from me my entire life, hoping cluelessness would prevent my powers from surfacing. While I still had a lot of questions about my childhood and the absentee mother who'd given me the witch gene, I was letting him off the hook. At least until he'd healed.

Once alone, I sat at my workstation, where I'd been spending a lot of time since my homecoming. I lost myself in my current creation: a silver mermaid brooch with a labradorite tail that shimmered in hues of blue, green, and purple. The iridescent stone was a favorite with tourists due to our area's renowned natural deposits. I was so focused I almost didn't hear the bell above the door tinkle.

Pulled from my trance, I removed my magnifying visor and went to welcome the customer. When I got to the front, they were backlit by the late-afternoon sun glaring through the windows, but the figure was distinctly female. Her slight silhouette floated from display case to display case as she leaned over them with curiosity.

I shielded my eyes. "Hello. Can I help you find anything?"

"Violet!" She flitted across the store to wrap her arms around me. It was Nolan's little sister, Kinsley. However, at twenty-two, she wasn't so little anymore. "I heard you were back in town. I'm so happy to see you again."

"It's been too long," I agreed, squeezing her back.

While the store kept me genuinely busy, I had to admit I'd been avoiding Kinsley since my return. Even though we'd kept in touch during my travels, I was afraid of how seeing her again would affect me. We'd been so close before Nolan's death, almost like sisters, and our time together lived in a special place in my heart: shopping trips, movie nights, answering the uncomfortable questions she couldn't ask her indifferent mother. Being five years older than her, I'd taken my unofficial big-sister job seriously.

It had felt strange to be ripped away from someone who was nearly family, downgraded to pen pals, especially after a tragedy that should have brought us closer together. Of course, it wasn't her fault or even mine, but I secretly wondered if her parents' hatred of me had influenced her over the years. If it had, though, I couldn't tell by the way she was beaming so genuinely at me.

I smiled back. "How have you been?"

"I have amazing news." She thrust her ring finger at me, nearly giving me a black eye with the baseball-sized diamond clinging to it. "I'm getting married." She squealed and did a happy dance. "His name is Lorenzo. We met while I was in Rome, and we're soulmates."

Laughing, I studied the ring. "Congratulations. His taste in jewelry is almost as impeccable as his taste in women. So when's the big day?"

She blew out a long breath, fluttering her blond bangs. "Four months from now. I know. It's so soon, but we didn't want to wait. Actually, the engagement is the reason I'm here. The ring is too big, and I'm afraid it will fall off and get lost. Could you please resize it for me?"

"Of course. When do you need it by?"

Gnawing her lip, she slid the ring off her finger. "I was hoping to have it for this Saturday. Daddy's throwing us an engagement party."

My mouth opened to say it was no problem, but I hesitated. Hadn't I been looking for a way to get closer to her father? A party with the whole family and all their dearest friends in attendance would be the perfect opportunity to suss out his feelings about Nolan's murder. Maybe I could even figure out what had driven him to stop looking for answers.

"Oh, no." Kinsley pouted. "It's too soon, isn't it?"

I shook my head. "I'll make sure the ring is done by then."

Clapping, she bounced on the balls of her feet. "Thank you so much. You're the best."

She laid the ring in my palm like it was a delicate butterfly, and I ducked behind the counter to grab the mandrel. I slid her ring down the long, tapered rod, checking the size: seven.

While I had her try on the different ring gauges to find the perfect fit, I wondered how to score an invite to the party. Surely, with all our history, an invitation wasn't out of the question.

I measured her finger at 6.5 and made a note on a pad of paper. "So is the engagement party a large event or a private family thing?"

"You know Daddy. He likes to show off. Practically the whole town is going to be there. Even Lorenzo's parents are coming from Italy, and…" Her gaze flicked to mine, and she pulled a face. "I'd invite you, of course. It's just that—"

"Your parents would rather die than put me on the guest list?" I filled in for her. "Don't worry. I understand." However, the disappointment stung, and not simply because I'd lost a chance to investigate. I wanted to be there for Kinsley during this momentous occasion.

"I think seeing you reminds them of what happened to Nolan. But I wish you could be there. It would mean a lot." She stared down at the display case, her focus distant. "Nolan would have figured something out. He was good at bringing people together. I miss him."

"Me too." Even though he made it difficult when he didn't leave me alone long enough to do so. However, being able to talk to him in death wasn't the same as living life with him. So close and yet so far away.

A moment passed before Kinsley's head snapped up, and she gave me a devilish grin. "We should sneak you in somehow."

I returned her mischievous look and tapped the countertop, thinking. It didn't take long before an idea stuck out, especially with Alice's predicament at the forefront of my mind.

"You probably already have a caterer," I began.

She pulled her lips to the side. "I imagine so, but I'm sure Daddy would make any changes I wanted. Why?"

I leaned closer. "Alice Wright started a baking business. She'd make you a real showstopper of a cake. And if you needed a couple of people to help serve it, Alice and I could assist." I batted my eyelashes innocently.

She narrowed her eyes. "That is so sneaky. I love it. How can my father say no? Especially if I don't tell him you'll be helping."

I tried not to take that the wrong way. "Exactly. I'll speak with Alice tonight and text you in the morning."

Using Kinsley to gain access to her father felt slimy. However, I really wanted to be there to celebrate with her, and there was nothing wrong with helping my BFF garner business at the same time, right? Besides, if she knew my real intention was to help her brother pass on to the next life, she'd be on my team. I wasn't about to go public with my terrifying ability, though. Not only did I want to avoid the subject, but I didn't want it getting back to Nolan's parents.

By the time Kinsley left the store, she was practically skipping. It was good to see her like that, so light and carefree. I wondered if I'd ever feel light enough to skip. I'd even have settled for a hop.

When I returned to my workstation, I abandoned my current project to resize the engagement ring. It was a simple yet stunning solitaire, so it didn't take long. No other customers came in for the rest of the afternoon, and once I'd locked up at closing time, I dove back into my mermaid project. I'd just finished polishing it when my phone dinged with a text. It was Dad, asking when I'd be home.

The antique wall clock said it was eight p.m. It was easy to lose track of time when I was in the zone, but what surprised me most was that Nolan had actually stayed away this long. Had he taken my plea for space to heart?

I responded to Dad, telling him I'd be home soon, then I checked for messages from Alice. There was nothing. Worried, I texted her.

A moment later, her response came through.

ALICE

I totally got that, but it sounded so depressing.

She sent me a smiley face, and I sent some X's and O's, but I knew my friend better than that. Alice was a classic helper. She liked to support everyone else but always refused aid when she needed it most. The least I could do was offer her some company.

I glanced at the time again. If I hurried, I might catch her at the bakery. She couldn't avoid me if I was there in person.

After cleaning my workstation, I shut down for the night. As I detoured from my normal route home, the streets were quiet, the shops shuttered for the day. Before I'd even turned the next corner, the evening breeze carried a faint scent of baking. However, it wasn't the usual enticing smells of cookies or cupcakes.

I wrinkled my nose and took another sniff: smoke.

My heart lurched, and I picked up my pace. As I neared Spread the Word, I squinted against the low-hanging sun. A tendril of thick, black smoke rose above the bakery.

It was on fire.

I sprinted for the storefront and pressed my face against the window. On the other side, water from the overhead sprinklers pelted the pane, streaming down in rivulets. I peered past them to scan the interior.

Please, don't let Alice still be in there.

Something sticking out from behind the counter caught my eye: a pair of legs sprawled on the checkered floor. And they weren't moving.

CHAPTER FOUR

"Alice!"

I banged on Spread the Word's window until my fists hurt, but the person lying on the floor inside didn't flinch. I tried the door handle. Locked.

Head swirling, I pulled out my phone, dialed 911, and reported the fire. The operator sounded infuriatingly calm.

"Help is on the way," she said. "Are you in a safe location?"

"Yes. I'm outside, but there's someone unconscious in there. They'll need an ambulance."

"It will be there soon. Hold tight, and stay where you are."

I tuned into the surrounding sounds, but no sirens pierced the air yet. It was quiet. Too quiet. No alarm blared inside the building, which would explain why the fire department hadn't been alerted. At least the sprinkler system worked, but would it keep the fire at bay until help arrived?

I searched for something to smash the window with: a rock, a trash can, a flowerpot. However, the touristy downtown core was too orderly. Everything was bolted to the ground or made of heavy wrought iron. Finally, I found a chair outside the coffee shop.

"I've got to go," I told the operator.

"All right. You can always call back if anything changes. Please, stay clear of the building."

"Sure thing." But I was already dragging the chair down the boardwalk.

Once I'd pocketed my phone, I braced myself before hoisting the chair. It was heavier than I'd anticipated. Grunting beneath the weight, I hurled it at the window.

Thunk.

Expecting shards of glass to rain down, I winced and threw an arm over my face. Instead, the chair bounced back.

I picked it up and tried again. This time, as it struck the window, cracks spread like spiderwebs across the large pane. On my third try, I swung it with everything I had.

Crash.

The glass gave way. A burst of warm, smoky air hit me, making me cough. Using the chair, I knocked out the remaining jagged shards that clung to the window frame and crawled through.

Blinking past the water droplets assailing my face, I raced around the counter and dropped beside the unconscious person. Enough light filtered inside that I recognized the youthful features from my frequent visits. It was Caitlin, the girl who'd quit earlier that day.

I shook her by the shoulders. "Caitlin!"

She was too still. I fumbled beneath her long, purple hair and swept aside a braided necklace. With shaking fingers, I searched for a pulse.

She was dead.

I snatched my hand away and fell back onto the floor. As I stared at the poor girl, fresh tears rolled down my cheeks, tears that had nothing to do with the smoke. Something made me reach out to hold her hand, maybe so I wouldn't feel so alone. Maybe so she wouldn't.

Sounds of sobbing drew my focus away from her. When I spotted a figure sitting on the floor by the cash register, I did a double take. It was Caitlin. Or rather, her ghost. The darkened interior made her look solid, but as she rocked back and forth, hugging her knees, she slipped in and out of the counter.

She stared at the tiles in front of her, muttering to herself between sniffs. The words were barely audible. "I'm sorry. So sorry. I shouldn't have done it…. take it back. I take it back."

Confused, I let go of her hand and noticed a silver ring on her finger that I'd been touching. I quickly laid a hand over it again, reforming the connection with her spirit. However, she didn't seem to realize I was in the room.

Keeping my hand on hers, I crawled closer to the ghost until I was in her line of sight. "Shouldn't have done what, Caitlin? Did you set the fire?"

She stared past me. "I'm sorry. I shouldn't have done it. Tell them I'm sorry."

While I was tempted to clap my hands or yell her name to snap her out of it, I didn't think that would help. "Is there someone in here with you? Is Alice in the back?"

She remained in a trance. I wanted to keep pressing her, but a high-pitched scream yanked my attention away. Was it Alice?

I turned to the kitchen doors. A warm glow flickered behind the windows set into them. Flames. As I stared, the light disappeared for a moment. Not like the fire was guttering but as though a person had passed by, momentarily blocking it.

Was Alice fighting the fire? Or worse, was she trapped?

I hesitated, wondering if I should perform CPR on Caitlin despite the fact her soul had already vacated the body. But someone in the back needed help, and they were still alive. For now.

Reluctantly, I left the young woman and shoved the kitchen doors open. A thick puff of smoke escaped, stinging my throat and eyes. I turned away to gasp for air before forcing myself to peer into the back where the smoke thickened.

Fire consumed a shelving unit along the wall. Flames licked

up the tiers, melting plastic bins and bags stored on them. Waterfalls of flour and oats poured onto the floor. The smell reminded me of the last time I'd tried to bake.

"Alice?! Are you in here?"

No answer. Groping the wall, I searched for a light switch but found none. My hand landed on something metal. A fire extinguisher. I trembled as I hauled it out of the holder and plunged into the dark, murky kitchen.

I focused on moving forward, refusing to think too much about what I was doing. But I wished Nolan were here—not that he could have done much besides lecture me for risking my life. Still, his presence would have been a comfort.

Something passed in front of the fire again. Was it a trick of the light? I squinted against the dancing flames. This time, I made out the shadowy figure of a person before they disappeared into the thick haze.

"Hello? Are you okay?!" I shouted then felt silly. Of course they weren't okay. They were caught in a fire. "Call out so I can find you!"

I ducked below the worst of the smoke, which was sinking lower to the ground by the second. With my watering eyes and the incessant sprinkler spray, my vision blurred. Thankfully, I'd been back there before, so I knew the layout. I felt my way deeper inside.

As I approached the inferno, my skin tingled from the heat, and the noise grew deafening. It was like listening to the applause of a crowded stadium, a staccato of crackles and sharp pops.

"Hello? Can you hear me?"

Maybe whoever I'd seen had already passed out. I didn't want to make that two of us, so I propped the heavy red canister between my legs and pulled the pin. Aiming for the flames, I squeezed the handle.

White retardant shot out. I wasn't ready for the nozzle's kick, and it jerked in my grip. Wrestling it back under control, I swept the stream at the base of the fire. The flames hissed in protest as I doused them. Soon, the canister lightened, and the blaze diminished, along with the heat.

I moved closer. And closer. My next step caught on something, and I stumbled forward. I glanced down to see what it was. A shoe. No. Not just a shoe. It was attached to someone.

A woman was lying facedown on the floor behind the island. A dark puddle pooled around her head. Blood?

I gasped then coughed as smoke scraped into my lungs. The extinguisher slipped from my hands, clattering to the ground as I scrambled to her side. When I brushed the dark hair away from her familiar face, I cried out.

"Alice! Alice, wake up!"

I laid a hand on her back. It rose and fell beneath my palm, and I almost collapsed next to her in relief.

A huge can of molasses lay nearby. Had it dropped on her? There was no sign of a ladder or step stool to indicate she'd fallen, but spinal injury or not, I had to move her. Since I'd abandoned my firefighting, the flames had grown again to lick the ceiling.

Carefully, I rolled Alice onto her back and hooked my arms under hers from behind. Before I could drag her toward the front, part of the shelf unit collapsed, blocking our path. I eyed the extinguisher, but it was almost empty. It wouldn't be enough to clear the way.

Doubling back, I hauled Alice toward the rear of the place, grunting and coughing and panting. We were halfway there when the alley door slammed shut with a clang.

I jumped, nearly dropping my friend as I whirled to face it. When I saw no one, I forged on through the hallway until my back hit the metal door. A giddy bubble of relief ballooned inside me, and I pushed. It opened a fraction then stopped. Something was blocking it from the other side.

The fire glowed brighter, and the smoke thickened, filling the vestibule. What time I'd bought us was up.

I set Alice down, stepped back, and threw myself against the door. This time, I heard a scrape, followed by a *crash*, and it swung open the rest of the way.

Fresh air rushed in, and I inhaled gratefully before regaining my hold on Alice. I pulled her out of the building and down the alley until my arms grew numb and my legs shook. When the sound of sirens filled my ears, I knew we were safe.

Once I'd laid Alice down, I collapsed next to her and watched the thick black smoke billow out of the bakery's alley door. While I stared, enough oxygen must have reached my brain because I finally noticed the garbage can lying on its side, its contents spread across the ground. That was what had blocked our exit.

I frowned as I noted the other cans and recycling bins lined up in a neat row against the wall some distance away. So how did one end up behind the exit? Then I remembered the door slamming. The overstuffed garbage can hadn't gotten there by mistake. Someone had placed it intentionally.

Fear rippled through my body as two things occurred to me. One, the fire hadn't been an accident. And two, someone had wanted to trap us inside with it.

CHAPTER FIVE

The sirens grew louder until they finally shut off, replaced by shouts that rose in the early night. While the emergency vehicles were parked only in front, I was too tired to call out and alert them to our location in the alley. As I lay on my back, muscles throbbing and lungs playing catch-up, I watched the strobe lights bounce off the smoke in the air.

"Vi?" Alice coughed. "Is that you?"

I turned my head to face my friend. "I'm so glad you're okay."

She tried to sit up but then winced and lay back down again. "What happened?"

"You were in the bakery when it caught fire, but don't worry. You're safe now."

I thought of poor Caitlin, who hadn't been so lucky. What had killed her? I wished I'd gotten more out of her shocked ghost.

I shouldn't have done it. Did she really have something to do with the fire? At first glance, she came off as a bit of a rebel—snarky attitude, purple hair, multiple piercings, DIY tattoos—but arson seemed extreme, even to get back at an awful boss like Roman. Either way, someone else had been in that building with us, someone who wanted to cover their tracks by trapping us inside.

Alice's eyelids drooped. I was no doctor, but I thought it best she didn't go to sleep.

I gave her a shake. "Stay with me."

She vibrated with shivers. Or it could have been me. We were soaked from the fire sprinklers, and the temperature was dropping quickly now that the sun had set.

Urgent footsteps echoed down the alley toward us. Two paramedics wheeled a stretcher in our direction.

"Over here!" I called, as if they'd miss us.

One knelt beside Alice to assess her. The other came to my side, but I shooed him away.

"I'm fine. Help my friend."

He looked ready to argue. In order to prove I was telling the truth, I struggled to my knees and then my feet. To my surprise, I felt better.

While they focused on Alice, I edged toward the bakery. I wanted one more peek before the crime scene was officially off limits. The smoke coming out of the door was less black and thick than it had been before. Voices drifted out, calm and measured. The firefighters must have put out the fire already. I took another step closer to peer inside and felt a crunch beneath my shoe.

I jumped back and scanned the ground. Something on the weather-beaten boards sparkled beneath the floodlight over the door. It was a silver charm so worn and faded, I could hardly tell it was supposed to be the letter "A." Broken chain links dangled from the end as though it had been part of a larger piece, perhaps a keychain or a bracelet. It called to me, so I picked it up.

The moment I touched it, my powers kicked into gear, locking onto an echo of the spirit clinging to the trinket. Vengeance hit me like a slap to the face. It was so intense and so specific that I knew it was aimed at the bakery. My magic left no doubt the item belonged to the arsonist, but was it Caitlin's, or did it belong to the other mystery person?

In a flash, the hostility vanished, replaced with a hint of kindness and warmth. It felt like a stranger smiling at me. However, if the person who'd dropped it was so good, then why had they lit a bakery on fire?

An impression was all I got. It wasn't as convenient as a movie playing in my mind, because having a power like that would be too useful. If I could have controlled my magic, I might have gleaned more, but that took practice—something I hadn't been doing.

Metal squeaked, and I turned to find the EMTs setting Alice on the stretcher. They looked hesitant to leave me. I wondered if I should put the charm back where I'd found it. But what if a firefighter's big boot kicked it into a gap between wooden planks? After a moment, I tucked it into my jacket pocket and followed the paramedics.

I walked alongside the stretcher and squeezed Alice's hand. "You're going to be okay."

The oxygen mask over her face muffled her response. I couldn't make it out, so I smiled back reassuringly.

As we headed out of the alley and around to the front of the shops, red and blue lights pulsed, bouncing off every window along the boardwalk. I squinted against the glare, peering at the chaos that had exploded in the street since I'd gone inside. Like fish to bait, nothing gathered the gossipmongers as quickly as sirens. It wasn't their fault, though. It was a Pavlovian reaction to any excitement in the small town.

Lucy rubbernecked behind the barricade in a stylish asymmetric dress as if she were standing on a red carpet on premiere night. She held her phone aloft, probably hoping to capture something gruesome to put in her article the next day. They said you should do what you loved, but Lucy loved a catastrophe a little too much.

Of course, some people might have flocked to the scene for

genuine reasons. In fact, I recognized most of those huddled behind the yellow tape as concerned store owners. With the buildings squished so close together and linked by streets made of old wood, the downtown core was a matchbox just waiting for a spark.

A head of bright, box-red hair stood out among the crowd, glowing even brighter when the emergency lights flashed red. It was Ingrid. While most of the onlookers' expressions ranged from curiosity to shock, hers held a glint of elation.

The threats and accusations she'd hurled at Roman earlier that day came back to me. It felt like too much of a coincidence that his business almost burned to the ground only hours after the altercation. Had she merely come to gloat? Or was she hanging around to admire her handiwork?

As the EMTs steered the stretcher toward the ambulance, I tried to keep pace but fell behind. Not wanting to hold them up, I waved them on and sank onto a nearby bench to rest. When I remembered my phone, I pulled it out. Thankfully, despite being damp, it still worked, and I texted my dad so he wouldn't worry if he heard about the fire.

A breeze blew off the ocean and up the street. Chills rippled through my body, and I shoved my hands into my jacket pockets—not that it did a lot of good, since even the lining was soaked.

While I sat, willing myself to move again, someone rushed up to me. It was the woman who'd recognized me in the bakery earlier that day.

Running her hands down the length of her long braid, she stared at the departing stretcher. "Is everyone all right? Was anyone hurt?"

I moved my head back and forth, but it wasn't a no. I just couldn't find the words to sum everything up. A young woman was dead, my best friend was on her way to the hospital, and a potential killer was on the loose. Everyone was not all right.

Heavy footsteps thudded toward us, and a commanding

male voice said, "Behind the tape, please." It was Jason—or Deputy Swan, as I needed to think of him.

With one last look at the ambulance, the older woman obeyed the order and scurried off. Legs shaking, I stood and faced my old friend. Handsome and confident in his uniform, he was the very picture of a man one could count on. However, the moment he caught sight of me, his authoritative expression fell away until the boy I'd gone to school with gaped at me.

"Violet?" He raced over. "What happened? Are you okay? Were you in the building?"

My soaked clothing, soot marks, and disheveled appearance must have answered his question, as he yanked off his jacket and draped it over my shoulders. Then he wrapped an arm around me to support my weight.

Grateful, I leaned against him. "I'm fine. It's Alice I'm worried about. I found her unconscious inside. I dragged her out, but I don't know how long she was in there."

Jason's face slackened, and he spun to watch the attendants load the stretcher into the back of the ambulance. The moment he spotted his cousin, his legs buckled until I wasn't sure who was supporting whom.

As though in silent agreement, we walked in that direction. While he stuck by my side, I could tell he wanted to move faster than I had the energy for. Jason and Alice might have been cousins, but they'd been raised together, making them practically brother and sister.

We'd nearly reached the ambulance when Sheriff Reed stepped in front of us. At the sight of me, his icy blue eyes narrowed, and his mustache tugged down into a frown. Considering his ongoing mistrust of me, he probably thought I'd started the fire.

"Hold on, you two," he said. "Let the EMTs do their thing. They seem hopeful she'll be all right, but the quicker they get her to the hospital, the better."

The sheriff was on the short side, but he had a sturdiness to his frame that said no one was getting past him. Shifting from foot to foot, Jason eyed the vehicle as though he was considering an attempt anyway. He must have thought better of it, because he inhaled deeply and some of the tension in his body melted.

He turned to me. "I hate to think what might have happened if you hadn't found her."

"Me too." However, I couldn't shake the growing feeling that if I hadn't pushed her to start Batch of the Day, Roman wouldn't have fired her, and she wouldn't have been in that burning building in the first place. "But I wish I'd arrived earlier. There was someone else in there. Caitlin. She… She didn't make it."

Jason shook his head. "Her parents are going to be devastated."

Reed's expression hardened. As he faced Spread the Word, he dipped his chin to his chest as though he felt weary. Or perhaps he was having a moment of silence for the young woman. I wished I could tell him what Caitlin's ghost had said, but the evidence inside and the autopsy would likely give them the answers they needed. Hopefully, it would turn out she hadn't set the fire. At least it might be a small comfort for her loved ones.

With a heavy sigh, the sheriff turned my way. "I'd like you to keep her death quiet until we inform her family. It will be better if the news comes from us rather than one of these looky-loos." He gestured to the surrounding crowd.

"Of course."

He tipped up the wide brim of his hat to have a better look at me. "Well, it seems you were very lucky tonight, but I think you should get assessed at the hospital."

"I'll drive her," Jason offered. "That way, I can check on Alice."

"Okay, but don't stay too long," he said, not unkindly, and

tossed over the keys to his SUV. "We have a lot of work to do here."

Jason steered me toward the cruiser. We were nearly there when a deep voice rose from those gathered on the other side of the caution tape.

"Let me pass!"

Roman Fedoro plowed through the crowd like he was playing a grown-up game of Red Rover. He tore down the tape and rounded the fire truck blocking the view. His broad shoulders sagged as he took in his precious bakery: the broken window, the smoke-blackened walls, water dripping from the ceiling. If he thought that was bad, he was going to be really upset once he saw the kitchen.

He gripped his slicked-back hair with meaty hands until it stood in rooster fashion. "No, no, no. It can't be. How did this happen?"

The sheriff and Jason tried to herd him back behind the perimeter. Roman brushed them off and wheeled around as if seeking answers. His search halted on the open ambulance doors, where Alice blinked groggily behind the oxygen mask.

He pointed a thick finger, surging toward her. "You!"

The sheriff's hand hovered over his holster as he barked commands Roman didn't hear. Jason grabbed the man's arm and dug his heels in. But as tall and fit as he was, Roman was dense with muscle, and his anger seemed to endow him with superpowers.

Alice shifted beneath the gray blanket. She struggled to lift her head off the pillow to see what the commotion was about. The EMTs slammed the doors shut before Roman got there, but he flexed his muscles like he might rip them clean off the hinges.

What did he plan to do once he got to her? Whatever it was, I wasn't going to wait to find out. Without thinking, I jumped into his path.

He came to a halt in front of me. Perhaps it was the

element of surprise or his disbelief that I'd even try to stop a charging bull like him. Either way, it worked.

As he aimed his bloodthirsty focus on me, I did my best not to flinch—or, worse, faint. After my adrenaline-packed adventure in his bakery, I was having trouble standing. A mere flick of his finger and I would have toppled over, but he didn't need to know that.

I placed my hands on my hips. "How dare you blame Alice. She almost died in that fire."

Roman snorted. "A fire of her own making. Sounds like karma to me." He whirled on the sheriff. "Aren't you going to handcuff Alice to that stretcher? She should be under arrest."

"Arrest for what?" I asked. "The only thing criminal was how you treated her today. She isn't capable of something like this. There isn't a vengeful bone in her body."

His guffaw was over the top. "That's what she wants everyone to think, but she threatened to get revenge on me. I have witnesses to back me up." He scanned the crowd before pointing at Ingrid. "You heard her."

The bread baker snickered. "You're on your own, Roman. Like I'd help you."

Any more than she already has, I thought bitterly. If only she'd kept Alice out of her squabble with him that afternoon.

Roman sneered and continued his search until he spotted Lucy. "You were there."

The reporter joined us, still recording with her phone. Her golden locks bounced as she skipped forward like the next contestant on a game show. "I can one hundred percent corroborate that."

I scowled at her. While I didn't expect her to lie, did she have to act so eager to throw my friend to the wolves?

Jason snapped his fingers at Lucy and pointed back the way she had come. "Behind the perimeter, please."

"What perimeter?" She glanced at the tape Roman had torn

and shrugged. "Anyway, I have footage of the entire argument. She told Roman, and I quote, 'You don't deserve my baking or the customers who eat it, and I'll happily take them from you.'"

Roman gestured wildly at his bakery. "And now, this happens? It doesn't take a genius to figure out who did it."

With a chirp of the siren, the ambulance pulled away, taking my friend with it. Wanting to be there for her, I was tempted to follow. However, it seemed I wasn't the only one, as Roman took an automatic step after it.

The sheriff blocked him. "The fire's out. There's nothing more to be done. Wait over there for us to take your statement." When Roman didn't retreat, he added, "I'm warning you. Back off and let us find the culprit, or you'll join them behind bars."

Though Reed was the shorter of the two, his badge must have held more power than Roman's thick biceps, because he backed away.

"As long as you do your job, it won't have to be done for you." He gave a dismissive sniff.

Jason crossed his arms. "Is that a threat?"

Roman raised his hands in surrender, suddenly too calm. "I don't need to threaten. Karma has a way of taking care of things."

The sheriff made a shooing motion at Lucy. "You can leave too. You know the rules."

"But I'm here in my professional capacity." She aimed her phone at him. "Any statements for me?"

"Yes." He looked ready to pick her up and carry her out of there. "Why don't you act more professional and less like a nosy neighbor? Nothing more at this time."

Pouting, she stalked after Roman, probably eager to conduct her interviews.

Shaking his head at the pair, the sheriff turned back to Jason. "You'd better take Miss Woods to the ER and check on

your cousin. I'll deal with Roman and get his statement before
'karma' takes matters into his own hands."

Jason nodded and led me to the SUV. When I sank into the
back seat, fatigue weighed me down despite the adrenaline
coursing through my veins. I'd just pulled my best friend out of
a fire. However, I was beginning to think it had only been the
frying pan, and things were about to heat up.

CHAPTER SIX

I paced the emergency waiting room, anxious for word about Alice. After the doc had given me a checkup and the all clear, the nurse shuffled me out; I couldn't even hear what was going on. Not only had my friend been knocked unconscious, she'd been closer to the fire and in the building for much longer than I had. How bad would her prognosis be?

If only Jason could have stayed with me. But while it had killed him to leave, he'd had a job to do. Now, all I had for company was a ghost in grease-stained coveralls who sat in one of the uncomfortable plastic chairs. Hunched over, he hugged his abdomen while rocking back and forth. It made me wonder if ghosts experienced pain.

"There you are!" came a voice from behind me.

Yelping, I whirled around. I hadn't heard the automatic doors swish open. As I spotted the figure racing toward me, though, I realized the sensor wouldn't have detected him.

Nolan instinctively reached out to me then clenched his fists and dropped them to his sides. "I heard the sirens and went to check it out. What happened? I overheard people say you were in the fire."

I looked around to see if anyone was within earshot—

anyone alive, that is. "Alice was inside the building. I got her out, but I don't know how she's doing. Can you go check on her for me?"

Not wasting a moment, he slipped through the avocado-colored wall. I resumed my pacing. Unable to keep my hands still, I twisted one of my damp red curls over and over until it regained its spring. Thankfully, it wasn't long before Nolan returned.

I rushed over to him. "How is she?"

"Shaken up, but she's alert and talking to the doctor. I peeked at his notes. There's not much to report since they're still running tests."

I slumped into one of the plastic chairs. "I hope they'll let me see her soon."

My head fell back, and I propped it against the wall. Relief and exhaustion pressed down on me until my eyelids drooped. Just as I began to nod off, Nolan spoke again.

"How's it going?"

My eyes flew open. "Huh?"

But he wasn't speaking to me. He stood across the room, chatting with the other ghost. While I was curious about him, I stayed put. We wouldn't have been able to converse without a piece of jewelry he'd worn when alive anyway. Helen had explained to me that, one day, I might learn how to hear ghosts without a conduit. However, that would take training, some-thing I'd get to eventually. You know, once I felt comfortable with the dead or pigs flew.

Now that the ghost was sitting up straight, the reason for his ER visit was obvious. Through a bloody hole in the front of his work coveralls, I glimpsed the back of his chair. Not because he appeared semitransparent beneath the fluorescent lights but because his torso sported a large hole.

I swallowed hard and averted my gaze, finding another limp curl to play with. When the man went back to hugging and rocking himself, Nolan gave up and sat beside me.

Leaning close to him, I whispered, "What happened to that guy?"

"He was in the cannery accident."

Although I'd been away for the last five years, news of a recent incident like that would have reached me. "Do you mean the one more than fifty years ago?"

People still talked about the explosion. It was part of our history, and since the cannery was Hope's largest employer, there hadn't been a single family unaffected by the horrific event.

Nolan crossed his legs, his argyle sock peeking out from beneath his pant hem. "The same one. He's anxious to see a doctor. I didn't have the heart to tell him it's too late."

"So he's been stuck in this room for half a century, and he doesn't know he's dead?" It seemed unfair he'd be waiting forever for help, bypassed by each new patient who walked in.

Nolan watched the cannery worker. "With ghosts, I think there are different levels of awareness. I wasn't exactly in the right headspace when I first died."

"I remember." I suppressed a shiver as I recalled the way he'd shadowed me, screaming soundlessly or watching me from the corner of my bedroom—just what you'd imagine a haunting to be like. "But you're not like that anymore."

"It took a while. Also, I think because I was aware of magic and ghosts before I died, it helped me gather my bearings faster."

I studied the man again, wondering about the hole in his chest. I'd never seen a ghost retain the injuries from their cause of death. Then again, until recently, I'd avoided lingering souls at all costs. Perhaps, because the cannery worker believed the injury to be a current one, it manifested in his physical, er... spiritual form.

"Is he in pain?" I asked.

Nolan tilted his head from side to side. "Yes and no. Ghosts can't feel physical pain, but he believes it's happening, so I'm sure it hasn't been a vacation for him."

"I'm surprised you've never seen him before. It's not as if there are a ton of ghosts in Hope."

His focus dropped to the linoleum floor. "I haven't been in this building since I died. It wasn't the best night for me."

I frowned. It hadn't been great for me either, but I wasn't about to complain, since I was still alive.

Suddenly, Nolan twisted in his seat to face me. "You should talk to him, try to help him move on."

Incredulous, I stared back. Sure, I'd helped Wyatt Thorn find peace, but it hadn't been easy. In fact, I'd nearly died. I didn't want to make a habit of that.

"What am I supposed to do? Track down a ghost doctor to pronounce him dead?" I knew I was acting flippant about a lost soul, but I was on edge, and being a literal spiritual therapist wasn't my priority at the moment.

"Look." He fidgeted with his cufflinks. "I know you don't love the power you were given, but you can't ignore it. You should use it to help troubled spirits."

Like himself? Is that what he was getting at? I didn't need the reminder I wasn't any closer to solving his murder than when I'd returned.

Before I could respond, the automatic doors hissed open, and the sheriff walked in. Jason followed close behind but slipped into the treatment area as though he had a backstage pass. Meanwhile, Reed homed in on me. Great.

As he studied my sooty face and soggy clothes, his gaze held less hostility than usual. "Miss Woods. How are you feeling?"

His almost human-like concern surprised me. "I'm okay. I wasn't in the building for as long as Alice."

"That's good," he said. "Because I want to ask you a few questions."

And here I thought he was worried about my well-being. Silly me.

He took out a notebook and clicked on his pen. "Start from the top, would you?"

I recounted the events of that evening, beginning from when I'd discovered the fire and then Caitlin, right up until the paramedics arrived.

He scribbled a note. "Did you come across anyone else while you were inside?"

"It was pretty dark and smoky, but I swear I saw someone when I first went into the back."

He scratched the scruff on his chin with the pen. "Could it have been Alice before she was knocked unconscious?"

"Maybe, but while I was dragging her to safety, the back door slammed shut. When I tried to open it, a garbage can had been placed behind it."

Reed looked up from his notes. "You say 'placed' like someone did it on purpose. Perhaps the wind knocked it over and it rolled in front of the door."

"Definitely not," I said. "It was filled to the brim and standing upright, away from all the other cans. It wasn't until I'd shoved the door open that it toppled over. Whoever was in there with us wouldn't have gotten out if it had already been there."

His eyebrow quirked. I couldn't tell if he believed my assessment. However, I was certain someone else had been in that kitchen, thanks to the metal charm I'd found. The one, I now realized, I'd forgotten to hand over.

A gasp escaped me. I pulled out the metal A, holding it by the broken chain so I didn't bungle the forensics any worse than I already had. "I found this in the alley behind the bakery. After Roman's blowup, I forgot I had it."

The sheriff released a long breath through his nose as he dug out a plastic bag from his pocket. "I appreciate your enthusiasm, but next time, try to avoid tampering with evidence."

Ducking my head, I dropped it into the bag. "I didn't know

it was important until I'd picked it up." I wished I could say exactly how important it was.

Considering how I'd interfered in his last case, I didn't blame him for jumping straight to "tampering with evidence." But in my defense, he'd been trying to throw my dad in jail at the time.

Sheriff Reed clarified a few more details with me before snapping his notebook shut. "That will be all for now."

He disappeared into the treatment area, probably to question Alice. I hoped they weren't too hard on her. She'd been through enough already.

Restless, I wandered around the waiting area. To pass the time, I browsed the health pamphlets, half reading them before tossing them back down again. When the sheriff and Jason returned, Reed didn't glance my way before he exited the building. Jason, however, gave me a grimace.

"I'm glad you're here," he said. "She needs comforting."

Before I could ask what he meant, the nurse stepped into the waiting room. She walked right past the injured ghost, who threw up his arms in frustration, like she was deliberately ignoring him.

"You can see your friend now," she told me.

Without waiting for a response, she left again. I dashed after her, but Nolan held back, maybe sensing Alice and I needed time alone. The nurse led me to the only bed curtained off, and I hurried inside the confined space.

With the head of the bed raised, Alice's pale face peeked out from under a heap of blankets. She was awake. An oxygen tube snaked into her nose, and an IV dripped next to her, but she looked better than the last time I'd seen her.

It seemed my friend was going to be fine. Relief overwhelmed me. That is, until she burst into tears.

"They think I set the fire. I'm going to jail!"

CHAPTER SEVEN

Alice buried her face in her hands, slim shoulders shaking with sobs. Each cry sounded like it scraped out of her, proving she hadn't come away from the fire unscathed. My heart ached at the reminder of how close I'd come to losing her.

I hurried to her side and leaned over the hospital bed to hug her. "You are not going to jail. No one believes you're capable of starting that fire."

She swiped at the tears that streamed down her pale cheeks, leaving clean spots in the soot marks. "Tell that to Roman. And after talking with the sheriff, I'm afraid he believes it too."

"I'm sure that's not true. It only feels that way when you're being questioned. He's just doing his job." I cringed as the words left my mouth. I'd been fed the same patronizing line when my dad was under suspicion. It hadn't been helpful.

Her watery gaze focused on me. "Sorry you got dragged into this. Are you okay?"

"I'm fine," I assured her. "I'm more worried about you."

"My head is pounding. The doc says I have a mild concussion and some smoke inhalation. Nothing too severe, so he'll probably release me tomorrow."

"So soon?" I eyed the tangle of hair wrangled into a loose bun on top of her head. "But there was so much blood."

She wrinkled her nose. "It wasn't blood. It was molasses."

I blinked, thinking back. "There was a can of it lying near your head. It must have leaked."

"I need a good shower and a bottle of industrial-strength shampoo, but it could have been so much worse. I'm alive thanks to you." The look she gave me overflowed with gratitude.

Seeing Alice in that bed stirred memories of the last time I'd been in the hospital, the night I'd lost Nolan. Tonight, the fire had nearly taken even more from me. I squeezed her hand to reassure myself that she was really here and not a ghost.

"What on earth happened in there?"

"I'm not sure." She stared at the rough blankets on top of her. "When I got to the bakery, I entered through the back door and headed straight for the bathroom, where the lockers are. I was in there for ten or fifteen minutes, so I don't know how the fire started."

"I'm surprised the alarm didn't go off," I said.

"You know how cheap Roman is. The system was old and poorly maintained. It wouldn't surprise me if he'd disabled it altogether since it was always alarming at the tiniest puff of smoke." She shook her head. "I only discovered the fire when I went to leave. It was small enough that the sprinklers hadn't activated yet, so I rushed for an extinguisher and… That's it."

"You can't remember anything after that?"

She touched the back of her head and winced. "I remember pain. The next thing I knew, I was lying in the alley next to you. It must have been the can of molasses that knocked me out, but I'm not sure why the new baker would store something so heavy on a high shelf."

Alice didn't even suspect foul play, as if the can had fallen on her by chance. "You're sure you didn't see anyone else inside?"

"No one. But I was in the bathroom for most of the time, and after that, I was so distracted by the fire I wouldn't have noticed a whale in the room." Fresh tears filled her eyes. "But the sheriff told me Caitlin was in the building. He said she died." She bit her quivering bottom lip.

I sank onto the chair next to the bed and held her hand. "Yes, I know. I found her."

"You did?"

"I… I was afraid it was you." An image of the legs sticking out from behind the counter rushed back to me, but I pushed it away. I didn't want to dwell on it anymore. I wanted answers. "Do you know why Caitlin was in there?"

"She often closed the store, so she had a set of keys. Maybe she planned to clean out her locker like me." Alice picked at the tape that kept the IV line in place on her arm. "Poor Caitlin. She just turned nineteen. The only reason she worked there was to save enough for traveling, and now, she's dead. She had asthma. I wonder if the smoke got to her and she had trouble breathing."

If that had been the case, why wouldn't she have escaped out the front at the first hint of danger? Had the attack been too severe, the onset of symptoms too quick?

Whatever the autopsy revealed, it meant whoever had set the fire wouldn't merely be facing arson charges but probably manslaughter charges too. If that hadn't occurred to Alice yet, I didn't want to break the news. She was upset enough as it was.

Instead, I explained what I'd witnessed: the backlit figure, the door slamming, the garbage can blocking the exit. "If either you or Caitlin forgot to lock the door, anyone could have snuck in while you were in the bathroom and waited around to knock you out."

Alice twisted the sheets as she thought. "What if they don't find evidence of anyone else? I'm the one with a motive to eliminate the competition or get revenge on Roman for firing me."

"Caitlin might have set it," I suggested, feeling bad for accusing her when she wasn't there to defend herself. "After all, she didn't leave under the best circumstances either. Maybe something went wrong, and the smoke overwhelmed her. And don't forget the mystery person I saw. They must have had something to do with it."

Alice huffed. "Oh, yeah? Prove that to the sheriff."

I will.

The moment the thought popped into my head, I was determined. While I hadn't been able to help Nolan the night he'd died, or ever since then, I could help my friend now. I'd solved Wyatt's murder and proved my dad's innocence, so I could unravel another mystery. But I kept my intentions to myself. Alice would insist she was fine and didn't need help. Not to mention, she already had enough on her mind.

"Don't worry," I said. "Right now, the most important thing is that you rest and heal."

"I can't afford to rest."

"You can't afford not to," I said in my best motherly tone. "You still have your savings to fall back on."

"About that..." She shrank until the bed appeared to be swallowing her. "Remember how I said I'd invested a lot in the business already? Well, I stretched myself too thin and spent nearly all of my savings."

"A-All of it?" My eyes widened. "On what?"

Alice let out a nervous laugh. "Appliances mostly. I can't legally use my home kitchen for the business, so I was setting up a commercial one in my basement. I bought an oven, a refrigerator, a mixer, and a bunch of other basics. When I got home today, I called to cancel everything, but it's too late. It all arrives in a couple of days."

I grimaced, imagining the bill. "Okay... well. Look at the bright side. You'll have what you need to dive headfirst into

Batch of the Day." I tried to sound as upbeat as Alice would if our roles were reversed.

She gave me a weak smile then sighed. "But it won't do much good without cupboards and countertops. I was relying on my paychecks from Spread the Word to pay for a carpenter, but now, that won't happen. And something tells me Roman won't give me my job back." She covered her face with her hands, muffling her hoarse voice. "What am I going to do?"

That was an excellent question. I was no baker, but a kitchen seemed pretty essential. And while I was eager to help Alice get her business off the ground, I was as useful with a hammer and nails as I was in an actual kitchen.

At the thought of construction, the person I'd been trying not to obsess about popped into my mind. A talented carpenter, in fact.

Max.

We weren't on chummy terms—my fault, not his. After everything that had happened between us, both in the past and since my return, was I really in a position to hit him up for a favor?

I released a slow breath and considered her other options. Reaching out to her parents wasn't among them. Her father had all but disappeared from her life when she was a child, and her mother lived halfway across the country, barely better off than Alice.

When I hadn't thought of anything to say, Alice flopped onto the stiff pillow as though all the fight—and hope—had gone out of her. "Maybe I should apply for a job at the cannery. Do you think they're hiring?"

"No!" My response came out much louder than intended.

The spirit in the waiting room was still fresh in my mind. While the cannery had likely improved its safety protocols in the last fifty years, I couldn't erase the image of his gruesome injury from my brain.

I cleared my throat. "I mean... They're always hiring

because people are constantly quitting. It's the worst job in town."

She shrugged. "At least it's something. Even if I got my business off the ground, no one would buy anything from me. By now, the whole town probably thinks I'm a criminal."

I perked up as I remembered my earlier visitor. Was it really the same day? "That's not true. Kinsley Abernathy came into the store today. She wants to hire you to bake a cake for her engagement party this weekend. And after a high-profile event like that, others will follow."

Alice narrowed her eyes in a tentatively hopeful way. "How do I bake that cake without a kitchen?"

My mouth opened, but no genius solution came to me, so I closed it again. I knew what needed to be done, even if I didn't like it. But this wasn't about me; this was about Alice.

"We might know a guy."

CHAPTER EIGHT

I white-knuckled the steering wheel as the car lurched into another pothole in the old forestry road—or at least I thought it was a road. It was so overgrown that it was hard to tell if those were tire ruts or animal tracks weaving through the thick undergrowth. Since Helen had been kind enough to lend Alice and me her sedan, I wanted to bring it back in one piece. I cringed as a twig scraped along the passenger door.

"Are you sure this is the right way?" Alice asked again. "It doesn't look like a road to a fancy resort."

"The place is still under construction," I said defensively. "I'm sure they'll have it paved once they open for business."

However, I had to admit I wished we had cell service to check our location, just in case we were lost. But I wasn't turning back now. Not after Lucy's article in *The Siren* had been released that morning, hot off the press. I hoped Sheriff Reed had gotten word to Caitlin's family because the two-page spread mentioned her discovered body. It also raised a few questions about Alice's involvement in the fire and death of her former coworker. If the stakes hadn't been clear the night before, they were crystal now.

Eventually, I rolled to a stop in front of a gate with a chain-link fence stretching out on either side. Dappled afternoon light filtered through the leafy canopy and onto a sign that said Private Property. I got out of the car to read the legal jargon printed in tiny font at the bottom.

Alice joined me. "Looks like a dead end."

"What? This?" I gestured at the sign. "There's nothing specifically saying 'Do not enter.'"

She raised an eyebrow. "They wouldn't have it barricaded if they didn't want to keep people out."

"But it's not closed all the way. Look, there's a gap. If they didn't want us inside, they would have locked it."

It was true. There was no lock, and the gate stood ajar as though the last person through hadn't fully closed it, but I was trying to convince myself as much as her.

While we contemplated trespassing, a tree branch overhead rustled, and something glided toward us. A tawny hawk settled on the top of the fence, head cocked at an angle to assess us. Its piercing gaze seemed to ask, *Are you sure you want to do that?*

I glared back. "Don't look at me like that. It's for a good cause."

Alice stared at me. "You realize you're talking to an animal again."

"He started it." I stuck my tongue out at the bird.

It blinked its intelligent blue eyes at me. Did hawks have blue eyes?

Alice sighed. "We should head back. We've already left Max two voicemails. Let's wait until he gets back to us."

Considering how Max and I had left things the last time we'd spoken, I wasn't so sure about that plan.

"He might be outside of cell service," I said. "We don't know when he'll call, and there's not much time before Kinsley's engagement party."

I'd texted the bride-to-be that morning, and she confirmed Alice was going to bake a cake for her party. She'd also informed me of the venue. It was the same place Nolan and I had held our rehearsal dinner the night he'd died. I dreaded walking back into the building, but I'd cross that bridge when I got there.

"I don't know." Alice wrapped her arms around herself. "I still feel weird asking him to build me an entire kitchen."

"You're old friends. He cares about you and will want to help."

Despite my attempts to justify trespassing, I'd normally have been the first to turn around. It was wrong. But so was what was happening to Alice. Helping her trumped any wrist slap I'd get. Besides, they really should have locked the gate.

I shoved it open and swung it wide. When we climbed back into the car, I drove through with more confidence than I felt.

"It will be fine. We're here on business, and we come bearing cupcakes." I thumbed over my shoulder at the container on the back seat. "No one says no to your baking."

Once we'd closed the gate behind us, we wound down the so-called road until the forest spat us out on the island's secluded west side. Seeing the messy construction site—parked equipment, piles of lumber, fencing—made me feel as though a piece of heaven was being stolen. However, I could already tell the resort was going to be stunning.

We parked outside a giant log structure that hugged the shore, expansive windows facing west to capture Charm Island's famous sunsets. Waves lapped at pillars that supported a deck where future guests might enjoy a five-star meal.

"This is beautiful," Alice breathed as we stepped out of the car. "I wonder if they'll allow the public to dine here."

"I hope they will," I said. "I love the Clam Shell as much as the next person, but sometimes, it's nice to dress up for something special. Maybe they'll even have a spa, and we can treat ourselves on girls' night."

Her posture sagged. "That's for people who have money and aren't in jail."

Before reading Lucy's article that morning, I would have

downplayed her concerns, told her she was probably worried for nothing. Now, I straightened with determination. "Right. Back to our mission."

I marched around to the other side of the building, where Max's boat bobbed next to a simple wooden dock, but there was no sign of him. In fact, there seemed to be no one around. A temporary Office sign dangled from the lodge's wooden railing. I considered popping in to introduce ourselves, but then the high-pitched *whirr* of a drill pierced the silence.

We followed the sound down the rocky beach to a group of cabins still under construction. I expected to hate them since so many locals complained the place would be an eyesore. But hardly any of the surrounding trees had been cleared to make way for them, and the structures' knotty log sides and green roofs blended them into the environment. It felt in harmony with the island's natural beauty.

The noise came from the third cabin in. I climbed the porch steps, the scent of sawdust growing thicker, and peered inside the spacious cabin. Max had his broad back to me. A flannel shirt hung around his waist over a pair of ripped jeans, and his muscles stretched his black band tee as he worked.

I paused to appreciate the kitchenette he was working on. In keeping with the aesthetics of the resort, the live-edge pieces showed every knot and flaw most woodworkers tried to avoid. Typical Max. Always going against the grain—pun intended.

Since there was no door, I called out, "Knock, knock!"

When he didn't react, I wondered if he'd heard me. Finally, he turned around and leaned against the counter he was working on. He didn't appear surprised, as if he'd been expecting me. Maybe he'd gotten my calls and decided to ignore me.

"What are you doing here?"

I stepped inside. "I tried calling, but you know, it's a Tuesday, and there's a breeze." As the local joke went, there was always some excuse for the poor cell reception.

His mouth curled at the corners. "Don't forget the clear skies and sunshine interfering with the signal."

Encouraged by the response, I stepped closer. "How have you been?"

"Good. Work has been keeping me busy."

"Yeah, I've noticed the *Crescent* missing from the marina for some time." I hoped it didn't sound like I'd been checking before work, after work, and on my lunch breaks. I had been, but I didn't want him to know.

Max gestured in the general direction of his boat. "Staying out here makes for a shorter commute. The landowner has been very accommodating. Speaking of which." He eyed me. "This is private property. Didn't you come across a closed gate?"

"It was open. Well… sort of. And it hadn't been locked."

"So you're a rule breaker now?"

I casually picked up a screwdriver from the counter as though I knew what to do with it. "I wanted to stop by. Thought we might catch up."

Exhaling loudly, he ran his fingers through his tousled black curls. "Look. I'm not sure what this is, but just because you're back doesn't mean everything has to be like it was in the past. In fact, I don't think things ever could be."

His words stung worse than I'd expected after all this time. He had a point, though. Here I was, trying to make it up to Dad and Alice for my long absence, but it was probably Max I'd hurt the most. Not only had we been friends for so many years, but there'd been something more between us, something we'd never been able to explore. And we certainly couldn't now, since my fiancé's ghost was practically glued to my hip.

A lump formed in my throat. "Right. You've changed. I've changed. People grow up and drift apart." Was that what he wanted?

"What are you really doing here, Vi?"

Giving up the pretense, I set down the screwdriver and

leveled with him. "I'm here to see if you have time for a side gig. It's not for me," I added, certain he'd shoot me down cold if that were the case. "It's for Alice."

I gestured to where she stood at the bottom of the stairs, hugging the cupcake container. When Max walked past me, he smelled of the forest, freshly cut wood, and hard work. It was intoxicating.

He stepped outside, squinting against the sun. "Hey, Alice. How's it going?"

She slapped on her happy mask. "I'm good. Great, actually. How are you?"

I knew she wouldn't ask for herself, so I stepped in. "There's no time to sugarcoat it. We wouldn't be asking for help if it was all roses and unicorn toots." I turned to Max. "Alice started a baking business. She's got all the appliances, but she doesn't have a kitchen to put them in. Her first gig is coming up, and I was thinking, since you're a carpenter and all, you might be able to help."

His expression grew unreadable as I rambled on. I didn't know why I'd considered this a good option. Likely because it was the only one.

When he faced Alice, it was with a much friendlier look. "What's your budget?"

"That's the problem." She toed the stones under her feet. "I lost my job at the bakery yesterday."

His eyes widened. "You're kidding. What was Roman thinking? He needs you. I'm sure he'll come to his senses."

"I doubt it." She kicked the stones harder as though to dig a hole she could disappear into.

Since Max had been out of town, it was possible he hadn't heard yet, so I explained about the fire, Caitlin, Alice's hospital stay, and how she was currently a suspect. I'd barely finished before he descended the stairs to give her a hug.

"I'm so sorry," he said. "How are you feeling?"

"I'm doing okay thanks to Violet."

He rubbed the scruff on his face as he stared out at the water, consulting something invisible. "When's your first job?"

"This weekend. It's Kinsley Abernathy's engagement party."

"Little Kinsley's tying the knot?" His eyebrows drifted to his tangle of black hair before drawing together. "That's a pretty tight deadline."

She handed him the container of cupcakes and backed away. "Yeah, you're right. It's ridiculous. We just wanted to check, but don't worry about it. Seriously."

Before she retreated any farther, a deep voice carried down the beach. "Good morning!"

We all turned to find a man in his early thirties heading toward us, loafers sinking into the rocky beach. He was dressed similar to Max, almost like he was copying his style, but his jeans were too stiff, and the plaid shirt had crisply ironed creases.

Max lifted his chin at the newcomer in greeting. "Trent. This is Violet and Alice." Then, to us, he said, "This is Trent Bass. The resort is his baby."

As we shook hands, I worried he'd ask how we got onto the property, but then Max held the tray of cupcakes out to him.

"They work for me. Cupcake contractors." He peeled off the lid. "Can I tempt you?"

"Don't mind if I do." Trent rubbed his palms together and plucked one out. "I wanted to check in and see how things were going."

Instead of choosing a treat, Max stiffened, all business. "I've completed the cabinet bases for fifteen of the cabins. I'm waiting for some hardware to come in, but I'm ahead of schedule."

Trent licked some icing off his lips. "I wish I could say the same. It's been one thing after another with this project. First, it was trying to convince the council to even approve it, and then, it was the permit delays and the strike. Now, some locals are protesting."

That didn't surprise me. I'd heard a lot of disgruntled rumblings about the place since I'd returned. "Well, it will all be worth it once it's finished. The way the buildings blend in with the environment is beautiful. Once people see that, they'll feel better about the resort. Grudgingly, but still."

He brightened at my comment. "Thanks. We've tried to minimize the impact on the location. I wanted to create a rustic yet elegant destination where people can get away from it all, really unplug, you know?"

I laughed. "With our terrible cell service and internet on the island, they'll have no choice."

"It's all part of the charm." Trent took another bite of his dessert, smearing some onto his clean-shaven chin. "This cupcake is delicious, by the way. Did you make these? You should do this for a living."

I pointed to Alice. "It's all her magic. She's famous for her baked goods. Just ask anyone in town. She actually owns a business called Batch of the Day."

Her cheeks turned rosy. "I only do cakes to order."

"For now," I added. "But she's planning to expand, and she's available for all kinds of events." I was getting pushy again, but my friend wasn't the best self-promoter.

Max's phone jingled in his pocket. After passing the cupcakes to Trent, he checked the call display.

So he does have service out here. That meant he'd definitely been screening my calls.

"Excuse me," he muttered then walked out of earshot.

Trent perused the other selections in the container before choosing a pink one with colorful sprinkles. "Tell me," he said to Alice, "would you be interested in steadier work?"

"What did you have in mind?"

"Once we open, I plan to outsource services to showcase local businesses, just like I hired Max to put his artistic spin on custom cabinetry. Guests don't want to come all this way to have the same experiences or eat the same food they can find back home. And let me tell you, I've rarely tasted something this good." He took another bite of cupcake, talking around it. "You should put in a bid for the contract. You'll be up against some fierce contenders, but I think you have a great chance."

Alice looked stunned. "Th-That would be amazing."

He produced a card from his pocket and handed it to her. "Email my assistant for more information. We'll need to know about your business and visit your facilities to see if you can keep up with the high demand of tourist season, but it's really just a formality."

"Right." Her enthusiasm waned at the reminder of her facilities.

Finished with his call, Max returned, work boots crunching on the stone beach. He cleared his throat to get Trent's attention. "It seems there's a delay in the supplies I'm waiting for. If you don't mind, I might head back to town for a few days. I've got a job I can squeeze in." He winked at Alice. "A kitchen project."

She gasped and squeezed his arm. "Thank you."

"Don't worry about it. I have an old set of cabinets I just removed from a renovation project. It won't be custom, but it will do the trick. And the local inspector owes me a favor, so he could probably assess it before the weekend."

"Sounds perfect."

Trent polished off the rest of his treat. "No complaints from this end of things. Like you said, you're ahead of schedule, and with all my delays, you'll finish long before the rest of the place is done." He turned back to Alice. "Before I forget, do you have a card?"

As she fished inside her purse, I leaned closer to Max and lowered my voice. "Was that really your supplier?"

"Nah. It was my mom."

I smirked. "You rule breaker."

"My supplies are late, so I didn't lie. In the meantime, I have other things to tinker with, but if Alice thought I was missing out on work, she'd never let me help her."

I pressed my lips together to hide my grin.

We made plans to meet Max in town and started to leave. However, with the kitchen problem dealt with, it freed my mind to return to the bakery fire. What Trent had said about the baking contract and fierce contenders made me pause.

I turned back. "Trent, out of curiosity, who else is in the running for the resort's baking contract? Or is that a secret?"

"There are only so many shops in Hope, so it's easy to guess. Spread the Word is one of them. They have a Parisian pastry chef, you know."

I battled to keep a smile on my face. "So we've heard." I didn't bother filling him in on the fire. He'd find out soon enough.

"I Knead Bread is the other. While they specialize in breads, they've promised to provide dessert samples." He chuckled. "Those two aren't shy about their rivalry with one another. The competition between them is really heating up."

"I bet it is," I said, mulling over his interesting choice of words. They made me wonder if the competition had heated up to the point of catching fire.

CHAPTER NINE

An electronic chime sounded as I entered I Knead Bread. Nutty aromas wrapped around me like a familiar hug, reminding me I hadn't eaten breakfast yet. I'd woken early and timed my arrival for just after opening to get Ingrid alone. Hopefully, I'd catch two fish with one hook: determine if she had any involvement in the fire and fill my tummy. Hey, I couldn't walk out of a bakery empty-handed.

A door to the back opened, and Ingrid came out, wiping her hands on her apron. She stood behind the counter, which spanned the width of the shop. "Morning. What can I get you?"

I scanned the floor-to-ceiling racks behind her. They overflowed with every bread product from rye to pizza pretzels. "How about a loaf of your nut medley bread?"

"Coming right up."

She snapped on a pair of gloves, plucked a loaf off the rack, and popped it into a bag before I could casually ask if she had pyromaniac tendencies. What had I expected? That she'd bake the bread right in front of me?

Gossip was my best bet to get her talking. After all, it was a favorite local pastime. "Pretty wild what happened to Spread the Word, huh?"

She punched the sale into the ancient cash register. "Sure is." Her tone didn't invite further discussion.

I reflected on her altercation with Roman, on how she'd sought support from his customers. And I was nothing if not supportive. "But I guess it's karma after what he did to you. I mean, who steals supplies from a fellow business owner?" I asked, not sure if I even believed the tale. "We're practically family down here at the boardwalk."

Now that the subject was about her, she turned away from the register. "Right? If you ask me, he had it coming to him."

I leaned in, like *Tell me more.*

She did the same. "Hope City has presented him with the Making a Splash award five years in a row. With all his scheming, it's no wonder." She straightened, a wary expression on her face. "Not that I resented him enough to seek revenge."

"Of course not. I'm sure he's made lots of enemies," I said, giving her an opportunity to cast blame on someone else.

Taking the bait, she lowered her voice, even though we were alone in the shop. "Alice isn't the only employee he's mistreated. Or woman, for that matter. Goodness knows he goes through enough of them."

My eyebrows shot up. "Roman is a ladies' man?" She'd hinted at his womanizing ways during their argument, but I couldn't believe women actually fell for him. I guessed he just wasn't my type.

"He likes to think so. He's destroyed more than one marriage in town. Even as we speak, he has two women on the hook."

I wrinkled my nose. "How does he manage that on an island?"

"You don't. Not for long, anyway."

Interesting. Once these women found out about his two-timing, they wouldn't be too happy with him. More to the point, what if they already had and the fire was the result? I wondered if one of their names started with an A, like the charm I'd found at the crime scene.

"Who are the lucky ladies?"

"I'm not sure. Rumor has it one is from Serenity." She sneered at the mention of our town's rival to the north. "And thanks to my location, I have a good view down Lobster Lane. I often see Roman going in and out of Mew to You, looking quite pleased with himself."

"You think he's dating Pepper Moon?" I wasn't sure why it shocked me so much. Stranger matches had been made. But there was something so genuine about the consignment store owner that I would have expected her to see right through a man like Roman, not be wined and dined by him.

Ingrid took off the gloves with a loud *snap*. "In a small town, beggars can't be choosers."

"Were you and Roman ever..." I made a vague hand gesture. "...together?"

She snorted. "He wishes. I used to bake for him, and that's all it ever was. He was awful to work for, but he promised to make me a partner in the bakery. Eventually, I realized he was full of hot air, especially after hearing about Grace Merriweather, the woman he opened Spread the Word with. Roman was the money, and she was the talent. Once the place was bringing in real coin—surprise, surprise!—he cut her out of the business on some technicality."

Roman had talked about making Alice a partner, too, at one point. Had she dodged a bullet? I didn't recognize his old partner's name, but if he'd cut her out of a business she'd helped build, that would be a motive for revenge.

"What happened to her?" I asked. "Did she open her own business somewhere like you did?"

"No. The poor woman died several years ago, broke and downtrodden, no thanks to Roman."

So that was a dead end. It still seemed likely the arson was connected to his way with women, though. It was possible the arsonist was a jilted girlfriend or a spurned husband.

The possibility of a male suspect jogged a memory. "I'm curious about the man in Spread the Word yesterday. Milton, I think his name was. Sounds as if he has a rocky history with Roman."

Ingrid waved it off. "Bad blood from a long time ago. Milton Curry is too nice to hold a grudge. Far nicer than Roman." She banged on the counter. "That man deserves his comeuppance."

"I think he's already gotten it," I said. However, it had been poor Caitlin who'd paid the ultimate price.

She shook her head of unnatural red locks. "The fire was barely a hiccup, thanks to his food truck. He's got his new baker, Colette, slaving away in that tin can. She's a Parisian pastry chef, you know." She must have forgotten I'd been there when he'd hired her.

"You don't say."

"Apparently, she baked scones today. Scones. Can you believe the disrespect? That's my territory." She appeared ready to march down to the sheriff's office and report her. "If you ask me, she's up to no good."

I nodded in support but didn't see how scones made Colette suspicious. "Well, hopefully, the whole ordeal will give you an edge on that resort contract."

"What's that?" Ingrid batted her eyelashes innocently. "Oh, that's right. I heard the resort wants a local to bake for them, but I'm a small operation and happy to keep it that way. I don't want to expand at my age."

Aha! Thanks to Trent Bass, I knew that wasn't true. Just when Ingrid had slid to the bottom of my suspect list, she jumped back up again. Why lie about the contract? To avoid looking guilty? Or perhaps it was only to save face if she lost to Roman. She could brush it off like she'd never applied in the first place.

When the door dinged, announcing another customer, I knew I'd teased out all the info I was going to get. Thanking her, I gathered my purchase and left. The visit hadn't crossed Ingrid's name off my list, but at least she'd handed me two more suspects: Roman's girlfriends. While I didn't yet know the name of the woman from Serenity, I thought some retail therapy at Mew to You was in order.

CHAPTER TEN

A loud *meow* announced my entrance into Mew to You. A Siamese cat glared at me as if to say *How dare you interrupt my nap.* I snuck past it, wanting to get some shopping done on my break. Okay, it wasn't my only mission, but purchasing something might butter up Pepper and get her chatting about her two-timing beau.

Weaving around display tables that doubled as scratching posts, I headed for the rack with the polka dot shirts that Alice and I had been eyeing. While she needed more than clothing to save her business, I hoped the new threads would give her confidence while working her first gig.

Finding her size, I swiped a few off the rack and carried them to the cash register. Pepper was already helping two other customers: a middle-aged man and a short, white-haired woman. The three overstuffed garbage bags that sat at their feet told me I'd be waiting a while.

Pepper hovered over the first bag and rubbed her palms together, a multitude of bracelets jangling on her wrists. "What treasures have you brought me today?"

The man dumped the contents onto the counter. "There might only be a few items worth putting on consignment. The rest you can consider a donation for your discount bin. I don't have space for it anymore."

As Pepper dug into the pile, the white-haired woman lunged to gather everything up. Or at least, she tried to. Her dark, age-spotted arms slipped right through the heap, leaving the clothing untouched. She was a ghost.

Squinting in the store's dim lighting, I searched for the signs I'd missed. There was a slight haziness to her form that I hadn't caught at a glance. For the first time, I noticed she wore a pink housecoat over a flower nightgown, the outfit she'd likely died in. A pair of fuzzy slippers completed the ensemble.

The sight of another ghost brought Nolan to mind. I hadn't seen him since the hospital two nights before. Had he taken the hint and given me a little breathing room? Or was he with his family, caught up in the excitement of his baby sister's upcoming nuptials?

After a few minutes, I shifted from foot to foot impatiently. The man ahead of me turned around, and I did a double take. It was Milton Curry.

He tipped his hat to me. "Sorry about this."

"No problem."

It wasn't like Pepper couldn't pause her treasure hunting to ring me through. But I hoped she wouldn't, since it was an opportunity to chat with a potential suspect. While Ingrid didn't think Milton held a grudge, she'd said a lot of things I had a hard time swallowing.

I gestured to the garbage bags. "Doing some spring cleaning?"

Pepper plucked a lacy bra from the collection, dangling it from her fingers to have a closer look. I instantly regretted prying.

Milton's brown cheeks darkened, and he hurried to explain. "That's my mother's. Er… was. She passed away last year, and I decided it's time to part with her things."

I frowned. "I'm so sorry for your loss."

The ghost gestured to herself as if to say, "What loss? I'm right here."

While I wanted to talk to him about Roman, I wasn't sure how to make the leap from deceased mother to their ancient history. Plus, considering how he'd reacted to Ingrid's teasing, I thought he'd need more coaxing than she had to open up.

Something drew my attention to the wooden box in his hands. Call it intuition or magical insight, but I was compelled to ask about it. "Is that your mother's jewelry?"

"Oh, this?" Milton hefted the box casually. "Just some bits and bobs. Likely all costume jewelry since my mom wasn't a flashy woman."

"Out of professional curiosity, may I have a look?"

He shrugged and opened it. I gasped at what lay heaped inside. Diamonds, emeralds, rubies, and pearls. Was that a canary diamond? They needed a good cleaning, but the collection was stunning. And he was going to drop them off at the local consignment store. It was like selling caviar at a truck stop.

My fingers twitched with the desire to touch them, but Mrs. Curry's spirit was still throwing a fit over her worldly possessions. I wasn't about to let my magic connect with her and tune into what she was saying. "You're just getting rid of these?"

"I'm an only child, so I inherited everything. As you can see," he gestured to the silk nightgown Pepper was assessing, "I don't have a need for most of it."

While the store had plenty of jewelry for sale, some worth more than others, Pepper also sold shapewear and orthotic shoe inserts. A collection this exquisite didn't belong there. While I didn't want to step on the toes of a fellow businesswoman, I couldn't help but intervene.

I lowered my voice. "You should have these appraised before you make any decisions."

Milton weighed the jewelry box in his hands like it was just one more thing to keep around the house. "I don't know. I'm already here, and Pepper's a great saleswoman." He watched her dig through the next bag with her round bottom in the air, somewhat appreciatively.

I doubted it was her salesmanship he admired most. "My father has a lot of experience appraising jewelry. He does it all the time for estate sales and people in your situation. We'll even do it for free. Please, just don't be too hasty."

He stared down at the box as though seeing it with new eyes then tucked it into the leather messenger bag hanging from his shoulder. "All right. I'll consider it."

The jeweler in me sighed with relief while my investigative side hoped it would lead to more alone time with him so I could coax out the story about his past with Roman. "Come by whenever you're ready."

One of the stuffed garbage bags rustled as Pepper wiggled halfway out of it. Before she dove into the next one, she glanced around like she'd forgotten where she was. "Oh, Violet. I'm sorry to keep you waiting. I'll ring you through quickly."

Just what I'd been afraid of. "Don't worry about me. I'll browse until you're finished. I'm in no rush."

"Don't be silly," she said. "I'll be a while yet, and I don't want to keep you from your shop."

Unable to find a compelling argument, I forced a smile and passed her the polka dot shirts. I'd have to return later to corner Pepper. Who knew investigations could be so hard on the wallet?

On my way back to Charming Treasures, I took a detour past Spread the Word—or what remained of it. I hoped to catch sight of Caitlin's ghost lingering around the place. If she'd had time to gather her bearings, she might be able to fill in some gaps with yes-or-no questions. And if not, maybe I could talk her through the confusion.

While plywood covered most of the window I'd smashed, I found a section of pane still visible and peered inside. The interior was dark, which made ghost-spotting a breeze, but I saw no movement inside. Had Caitlin's spirit moved on, or was she still rocking herself behind the counter?

I was tempted to check if the alley door was unlocked, but I couldn't risk getting caught sneaking around the place; my association with Alice would only make things worse for her. Besides, I didn't need powers to know I was making progress in my search. Who needed magic when I had twenty-seven years' experience being a resourceful human?

When I reached the promenade, I spotted Spread the Word's food truck parked next to the railing that looked down on the marina. The lineup of customers snaking from it was longer than I'd ever seen at their storefront. I wondered if the shop being on wheels gave people the impression of scarcity, like the treats might drive away at any moment. Since I hadn't found my footing in the investigation yet, I thought it wouldn't hurt to meet the mysterious new baker who'd arrived in town the moment trouble had.

Okay, so my mistrust of the pastry chef was flimsy, but bumping my best friend out of a job hadn't earned her any brownie points with me. Out of loyalty to Alice, I secretly wanted her to be guilty of something, if for no other reason than to stick it to Roman. If nothing else, I was curious to find out if she was any good at baking or if there was still a chance Roman would beg Alice to return.

Joining the line, I watched Colette work in the back of the boxy white truck. As she leaned out the large side window and took a customer's order, she shoved limp curls away from her flushed face. Although it was still spring, and the green-and-white-striped awning protected her from the sun's rays, the truck would have trapped the heat like an oven. Somehow, her disheveled appearance made her even more attractive.

She packaged orders and returned change in an efficient manner, and the line moved quickly. Several more people joined the wait behind me, which meant I wouldn't get much time to question her. I stayed anyway, enticed by the smells wafting out of the truck—not that I would have admitted that to anyone. Especially Alice.

When it was my turn, I was ready for something sweet. Mouth watering, I peered into the glass display below the counter Colette leaned on. There weren't many options left.

"What do you recommend?" I asked her.

"We are low on selection. Roman should return soon with more from the bakery, but if you are in a hurry, I think the lemon scones are the best." She pointed to the pale triangular treats drizzled in a semiopaque glaze.

Risking the wrath of Ingrid, I ordered a few to share with my dad. As she prepared a box to place them in, I struggled to come up with small talk. However, Colette beat me to it.

She pointed her tongs at me. "You are the friend of that baker, the one I replaced, no?"

I guess we were skipping the small talk. "Yeah. I'm Violet."

"And you are buying pastries from me?"

She didn't introduce herself. I already knew her name, but still, her candor was jarring. I wasn't sure if it was a French thing or a she-didn't-like-me thing, but I couldn't complain when I was on a time crunch to gather intel.

I followed her direct lead. "I thought I'd check out the competition. How are you liking the job so far?"

"Working in this monstrosity was not what I had expected when I applied. But *c'est la vie*. Roman says he will rebuild as soon as the investigation is done." She brushed a sweaty curl off her forehead. "I am looking forward to some air-conditioning."

"Hopefully, the bakery will be up and running before the

weather gets too hot," I said. "Where are you baking out of now?"

She lifted a shoulder. "The damage was not so bad. Only one part of the kitchen was burned. They say it is safe, so I can use the back entrance and work around it." She held out her hand for payment.

It seemed I was running out of time, so I slowly took out a bill from my wallet. "Can I ask, with all of your experience and skill, why move to such a remote village?" I was laying it on thick, but flattery couldn't hurt, right?

Colette appeared pleased. "It is true. I am skilled, but it is difficult to stand out in Paris, a city filled with the best bakers in the world. There is a pâtisserie on every corner, and everyone has a family recipe for macarons. I wanted to go somewhere my talents would truly be appreciated."

"A big fish in a small pond."

"*Oui*, exactly." She passed back my change and held out the bag of scones. "When I was doing my research, I learned there will be a world-class resort built here. I knew I could make a mark, so I found the only bakery in town to offer my services. Now, here I am—how do you say—living the dream." She gestured at her metal prison.

I took the bag from her. "Like you said, it won't be for long. I'd wish you good luck, but I don't think you need it."

"*Merci*."

Someone behind me cleared their throat. My time was up. I hadn't coaxed much information out of Colette, but it was possible there was nothing to get.

Knowing I might not get another face-to-face conversation with her, I stuck out my hand. "It was nice to meet you. Welcome to Hope."

"Ah, yes. You Westerners and your handshakes." Colette held out her hand limply.

Since she was standing in the back of a truck, I pretended

to struggle with the height difference. Overextending, I let my fingers graze her bracelet and reached out with my powers.

A clear sensation ran through me. It was cold and determined, with a confidence that bordered on arrogance. Unfortunately, it was nothing like the broken trinket I'd found in the alley behind the bakery. Thanking her, I left.

As I made for the jewelry store, I peeked inside the bag. The smell was too tempting to resist, so I pulled out a scone and took a bite, really wanting to hate it. But it was delicious.

Ingrid might have been suspicious about Colette, but how much of that was jealousy? Or perhaps it was because, as a stranger, the pastry chef was an easy target to thrust suspicion onto—and off Ingrid herself.

Colette had no motive to burn down the place that had just hired her. She hadn't been working there long enough to get fed up with Roman's charming ways, and now, thanks to the fire, she was stuck working in a food truck, which she wasn't pleased about. As much as I wanted to dislike her, her only fault was moving to a new town and applying for a job.

When I reached Charming Treasures, I jammed the last bite of scone into my mouth, pausing a moment to savor it. Unfortunately, my extra carb stop had revealed one thing: Alice would not be getting her job back anytime soon.

CHAPTER ELEVEN

Seated at my workbench, I was poised with a torch in my hand, ready to solder a filigree embellishment, when Dad cried out behind me. I jumped, nearly burning myself, and turned around. He stood stock still as Zelda coiled around his leg, purring.

His expression was one of horror, like she was a black python about to squeeze the life out of him. "I don't know how she keeps getting in. No one has come or gone. I swear she can teleport or something."

That probably wasn't far from the truth. "Maybe she snuck in with us earlier and has been napping all this time."

He seemed to accept this explanation, because the alternative was too weird if true. "Well, I wish she'd stop jumping out of the woodwork. She scared me half to death."

The cat slid her sharp gaze to me, a mischievous glint in her eyes making it obvious that was exactly what she'd intended.

I bit back a grin. "I guess when you have nothing better to do than lick your nether regions all day, you entertain yourself however you can. We should put a bell around her neck."

Zelda made a noise like she wanted to maul me. *I'd like to see you try.*

To Dad, who was oblivious to the familiar's telepathic abilities, it must have sounded like a cute cat noise because he bent over and scratched a spot behind her left ear. Her threat forgotten, she closed her eyes with pleasure and arched so he'd hit all the right spots.

"So, how is Alice doing?" Dad asked.

I sighed. "She's staying busy to keep her mind off things. Max built her a kitchen with some cabinetry he had from an old job, so she can bake for tomorrow night's party."

"That was nice of him. Is the sheriff still harassing her?"

"A little here and there, but there's been no news about the investigation." I pulled my lips to the side. "Which is both good and bad, I suppose."

He straightened, readjusting the sling that held his casted arm. "Well, Alice is innocent, so I'm sure it will all work out."

It took everything I had not to roll my eyes. He'd said the same thing when the sheriff was after him for murder, and that had only worked out because I'd solved the case. But Dad preferred optimism over realism. Maybe that was why he continued to accept my weak excuses for Zelda's bizarre behavior.

The bell above the front door rang as a customer came into the store, and he moved to see who it was.

"I'll handle it," I told him. "Why don't you take the rest of the day off?"

It wasn't as if I had any new leads to chase anyway. I'd stopped by Mew to You again the day before, but a note on the door said Back in Five. I'd waited fifteen before leaving.

Dad shrugged and moved his casted arm as though testing out a new shirt. "Actually, I feel pretty good today. I think I'll come back."

"Glad to hear it. Enjoy a long break, though."

He gave Zelda one last pet then disappeared into the front,

pausing to greet someone before he left. When I poked my head out, I was thrilled to find Milton—not just because he'd listened to my advice but also because I was relieved to regain some momentum in my investigation. I was less thrilled, however, to see his mother.

Mrs. Curry followed her son into the store, stomping her fuzzy slippers. She seemed even angrier about this trip than the one to Mew to You the day before. I couldn't blame her. Today, Milton wasn't looking to sell her old bras but her precious jewelry.

Zelda padded out of the back, which she often did when customers came in. I always wondered if it was more for the attention she'd receive or because she enjoyed making snarky remarks about them that only I was privy to. However, upon seeing the ghost, she muttered something under her breath and raced into the back again. I wanted to do the same.

"Hi, Milton. I'm so glad you came in."

He set the simple jewelry box on the counter. "I considered what you said and realized my mother didn't wear much jewelry, so if she kept these, they must be important."

Mrs. Curry turned her palms, and eyes, upward, like *No kidding*.

I pulled out several velvet trays and laid them on the countertop. One by one, he set each piece of jewelry on the soft fabric. I would have done it myself, but I wasn't ready to hear what his mother had to say. While the gemstones didn't sparkle as they should and age had tarnished the metal, their quality was obvious.

"They're beautiful," I breathed.

He leaned closer, probably trying to see what I did beneath the years of dust and grime. "If they're not costume jewelry, then I'm not sure where they would have come from."

Studying the pieces closer, I noted the hallmarks and craftsmanship. "They appear antique. Perhaps they were passed down through the family."

One necklace grabbed my eye. No, that wasn't right. Not my eye so much as my magic. Something familiar was calling to me. Unable to resist, I picked it up.

The disgruntled mutterings of Milton's mother became audible, as though someone had turned up her volume. "Get your greedy hands off my things."

I ignored her, not wanting to tip her off to my power. Reaching out with my magic, I peeled back the layers of spirits who'd once worn the necklace. Mrs. Curry's sparkling personality was there at the top, followed by the women in her family who'd owned the jewels before her. However, beneath that, like a subtle hum or whisper, was the artist's presence, and I felt a kinship with him.

"My great-great-grandfather made this," I said almost to myself.

"Really?" Milton asked. "How can you tell?"

"Er…" I jerked back to reality, reminding myself I wasn't alone. "Every artist has their own particular style." Then I located the tiny mark on the back of the setting. "And see here? He initialed it 'A.W.' Abram Woods."

"Amazing. Then it's fitting you'll be evaluating it."

"Well, my dad will. I still have a lot to learn from him." I continued to hold the necklace, not ready to release the connection to my ancestor. "Do you mind if I ask what you plan to do with the jewelry?"

"I guess I'll sell it."

Mrs. Curry clutched her generous and semitransparent chest. "Oh, my heavens. I just rolled over in my grave. You can't possibly sell those."

While I was tiring of the dramatics, I had to agree with her. "These are heirloom quality and are in beautiful condition. Are you sure you wouldn't want to hold on to them? You could pass them on to your children."

He ducked his head of thick white hair. "There's no one to pass them on to. I'm fifty-eight and have no kids."

Mrs. Curry fanned her fingers in front of her eyes as if fighting tears—even though ghosts didn't have tear ducts. "You don't need to remind me. All I ever wanted was to be a grandmother. Apparently, that was too much to ask."

While it was a shame to let all that family history go, I didn't know his reasons for wanting to sell. His mother's possessions might have been too painful a reminder to keep around. Or else he needed the money. The pieces would fetch a tidy sum if sold through the right channels. Once again, I was glad I'd caught him before he'd dropped them off at Mew to You.

I set the necklace down and picked up the canary diamond ring. "How about holding onto this? You never know when *the one* will come along. What woman could say no to this masterpiece?"

His mother snorted. "Fat chance. He hasn't had so much as a girlfriend in years."

Milton rubbed the back of his neck as if he sensed her gaze boring into him. "I've never had much luck in that department either. Doubt it's improved with age."

Mrs. Curry continued to nag him the way she probably had all his life. "I thought you'd end up with that one girl, but you let her get away. Could have moved on, but did you? No."

Her snide comment brought to mind Ingrid's teasing. "Is your bad luck what Ingrid Larsen was talking about in the bakery the other day?"

Milton's chuckle was a pleasant sound, deep and congenial. "Yes. However, it wasn't so much bad luck as it was Roman." He went quiet, staring at the ring I held.

His mother spat on the hardwood floor, which, thankfully, wouldn't need cleaning. "Blame that cad all you want. You let her slip right through your arms and into his."

After a moment, he cleared his throat. "But that was a long time ago. All water under the bridge. Though not much has changed for Roman. He still treats women like they're disposable. Even now, he has two girlfriends."

Mrs. Curry huffed. "And here you can't even get one. If you'd go out now and then, actually talk to a woman, you might stand a chance."

"Do you know who the two women are?" I asked.

Milton fidgeted with his shirt collar. "I shouldn't have brought it up. It's none of my business."

Since Pepper was one of those women, the eyes he'd been making at her told a different story. However, he didn't strike me as the usual town gossip, so I didn't pry it out of him.

"Don't worry," I said. "I already knew about his love triangle." But if yet another person in Hope was aware of it, there was an even better chance the girlfriends did.

Getting to work, I snapped photos of each item and uploaded them to the computer. After I created a document that itemized what he'd brought in, I printed it off and handed him a copy.

The jewelry tinkled as I began rearranging the pieces. "I'll have my dad assess these, and we'll get back to you within a couple of weeks."

"Thank you. I appreciate it." He made to leave but then paused. "Next time you see Alice, tell her I say good luck with the new business. I hope it won't be too long before I taste her doughnuts again."

As he left the shop, his mother followed on his heels, barking at him. "If you sell those jewels, I swear I'll learn how to move things. I'll drop a piano right on your head."

I wasn't sure how many pianos were being moved through second-story windows around town, but she seemed to mean it. I wished there were a way to warn him. However, if he'd survived the woman in life, I was certain he could endure her abuse now that she was dead.

Shaking my head, I took the jewelry into the back. As I locked it away in the wall safe, my thoughts turned to the arson. So far, my investigation wasn't pointing to any person in particular, but to cover my bases, I needed to find out who

Roman's second girlfriend was. And it wouldn't hurt to learn more about the man himself.

Zelda jumped down from her hiding spot on my workbench. She stretched with her furry butt rising in the air and nails scratching the hardwood floor. As she headed for the door, Dad's comment about the cat came back to me and gave me an idea.

"Zelda, how do you come and go through closed doors?"

She quirked an eyebrow. *We all have our skills. At least I'm not foolish enough to take mine for granted, like you.*

"Don't you start. Helen and Nolan already lecture me enough. Did they put you up to giving me a hard time too?"

I don't need their encouragement to call you foolish. Witchcraft isn't a knitting project you can put down and come back to. Unchecked magic is dangerous. The longer you wait, the harder it will be to control.

Maybe that was the reason Helen had moved in next to us after my mom took off, to monitor the seven-year-old ticking time bomb. "Okay, okay. But right now, my priority is to clear Alice's name, and I'd accomplish that faster if I had your help. How do you feel about doing some reconnaissance at Roman's house?"

Zelda narrowed her eyes. *You want me to break into someone's place?*

It was difficult to tell if she was appalled or intrigued. "You could just look around. I'm not asking you to be a cat burglar."

The feline raised a paw. *Please, hold the cheesy jokes if you don't want to find a hairball in your shoe tomorrow. I wasn't judging, only clarifying. I have no problem breaking into houses. It's nothing new to me. Laws are meant for humans, not cats.*

I thought if lawmakers knew about this particular cat, there'd be a few amendments.

So? she asked. *What's in it for me?*

I crossed my arms. "Didn't Nolan ask you to help me out, keep an eye on me as a favor to him? I didn't realize that involved manipulation."

Her whiskers twitched. *It's not manipulation. It's quid pro quo. Have you forgotten I'm not your familiar? If I'd known I'd be stuck as your substitute, I'd have happily plunged off that cliff with Nolan. But with my luck, I'd be trapped as a ghost, still helping the world's most useless witch.*

I ignored the insult, too busy trying to remember if I'd ever seen an animal spirit. "Cats can become ghosts?"

Zelda huffed, which sounded like she was bringing up that hairball she'd mentioned. *How rude. Contrary to popular belief, we have souls, too, you know. All animals do.*

"Of course. I didn't mean to imply—"

As it happens, a cat's unfinished business usually involves chasing a bird or finding the best ray of sunshine to lie in for their eternal sleep. They pass on quickly. I'm not just a cat, though. I am a familiar. She flicked her tail. *If I become a ghost, I will haunt you for the rest of your life. Remember that next time you forget to feed me and I nearly die of hunger.*

By the looks of her expanding midsection, I doubted she was at risk of that happening. I suspected she'd been begging Dad for food on top of what I fed her, but whatever kept her happy. Or at least less miserable.

"Right. So does that mean your payment involves food?"

She lifted her chin. *It might.*

"How about an extra can of tuna for the next few days?"

The next week. She turned and sauntered into the back. *And make it the expensive kind.*

CHAPTER TWELVE

As I stalked in front of the bay window in our living room, I spied through the curtains. I didn't know what I expected to see. It was nighttime, and I was waiting for a sleek black cat and a ghost, so unsurprisingly, there was no sign of them. Letting the curtain fall back, I resumed my pacing while I tugged on a stray lock of hair.

Dad folded his newspaper and lowered the recliner's footrest. "Who are you waiting for? Is Alice coming over?" Clearly, my anxiety was getting to him.

"No." I didn't expand on my answer. Talking with him about witch stuff still felt weird.

"Are you going out with someone?" He gestured to my outfit.

Dressed in my black leather jacket, black jeans, and black boots, I supposed I looked ready for a dive bar. Or a vampire-slayer convention. "My plans changed, so I'm staying in tonight."

I'd wanted to accompany Zelda when she broke into Roman's house—or whatever the cat did to get into places. However, Nolan had made an appearance and put a stop to it, threatening to haunt me if I did. Zelda must have ratted me out.

Okay, he'd made some good points. If someone caught me near that house, how would I explain why I was hiding in the bushes, wearing burglar attire? Plus, what was I really bringing to the team—moral support? After catching him up on everything I'd learned so far, I asked him to stop by Spread the Word following the break-in to check on Caitlin. Maybe he'd get more out of her than I had.

I peered outside again. When I saw nothing, I spun back to face Dad. This time, however, he wasn't alone. Nolan stood behind him, having come in as quietly as a… well, a ghost.

I gasped, causing Dad to jump. A second later, Zelda slipped into the room and leaped onto his lap. He practically fell out of the chair in fright. Poor Dad.

Once the shock had worn off, he recovered and scratched behind her ears. "I don't know how you do that," he admonished her.

Unable to wait another moment, I addressed the two spies. "So? What did you find out?"

Dad blinked. "About what?"

"Sorry. I was talking to Zelda and Nolan."

His hand froze mid-pet as though realizing an alligator had sat on his lap. It was exactly why I didn't talk about magic with him. But I didn't care at the moment. I needed answers.

Zelda shoved her head beneath Dad's palm, forcing him to resume his pets. She regarded me through half-lidded eyes. *I believe we had a deal. Now, it's your turn to keep your end of the bargain.*

Though I was ready to explode from suspense, I threw up my hands in surrender. "Fine. Follow me."

Dad shifted in his recliner. "Where?"

"Sorry. Not you. You're good."

Zelda vaulted off his lap and padded toward the kitchen. By the time I got there, she was pawing at the cabinet I kept the tuna in.

I pulled out a can. "You can magically get into locked houses, but you can't open a cupboard door?"

What would be the point? It's not like I can open a can without opposable thumbs.

"Fair enough."

I considered giving her half now and half after I got the intel but decided the risk of a clawing wasn't worth it. Once I'd cracked open her treat, I scooped the mushy mess into a bowl and set it on the kitchen tiles.

The floor? How's that for hospitality? But she began devouring it anyway.

Nolan and I moved to the dining table nestled in the kitchen's rounded nook. When I pulled out a chair for him, he unbuttoned his suit coat before sitting. Silence settled over us except for the loud chewing sounds coming from the kitchen floor.

When I couldn't listen to the wet noises any longer, I asked, "Did you end up finding Caitlin's ghost?"

He shook his head. "No. I searched the whole bakery and even stopped by her house to see if she was hanging around her parents, but there was no trace of her."

"Thanks for trying."

Disappointment welled inside me, but I figured she'd turn up eventually. If she'd been responsible for that fire in any way, the guilt couldn't be resolved after a few days.

As the silence dragged on, I turned to a lighter subject. "How is your family?"

He beamed, happier than I'd seen him since… well, since before he'd died. His sister always had that effect on him. "They're excited. Everyone's in a frenzy over the engagement party: making calls, booking flights for family, sending last-minute invites. Practically everyone in town is invited."

Not everyone, I thought.

His cheer evaporated, and his chin sank to his chest. "I'm happy for Kinsley. I just wish I could be there."

"You'll be there in spirit." I grinned. When he didn't respond, I ducked my head to catch his attention. "Get it? Because you're an actual spirit?"

"Is this your version of a pep talk?"

"Yup. How's it working?"

The look he gave me was flat, but the corners of his mouth quivered as he fought a smile.

"Actually, I'll be at the party too." I tried to sound super casual about it. "I'm going to help Alice serve the cake she's baking for the event."

He squinted one eye at me, likely wondering why special cake servers were required when the Abernathys had probably hired the best event coordinator money could buy. I didn't want to get into it. Thankfully, Zelda hopped onto the chair next to Nolan, saving me.

We both stared at her expectantly. She held my gaze for several seconds before thoroughly cleaning herself.

Tapping my foot, I waited as long as I could. Then I snapped. "Can we begin already?"

"Yeah," Nolan agreed. "Let's get on with it. You're killing us here. Well, you're killing Vi, at least."

The cat's gaze bored into me for another beat before she gave herself one more lick to show who was boss. She planted both paws on the table and stood on her hind legs, like a bartender leaning against a countertop.

We didn't find a lot. Roman's got a minimalist vibe to his place. No keepsakes. No mementos. For as much as he collects women, there seems to be no evidence of them left behind except for one photo.

"Who's in the photo?" I asked.

The cat's furry shoulder rose. *A woman. I don't recognize her, but most humans look alike to me. Ugly, with too much exposed skin.* She shuddered. *It makes me cold just looking at you. But I can show you the picture in case you know her.*

My mouth popped open. "You stole it? So you are a cat burglar."

She slapped a paw to her forehead. *Again with the terrible puns. I meant like this…*

One moment, I was staring across the table, and the next, a face swam before me. It was an aged photo of a young blond woman, maybe around twenty years old, with freckles across her nose and a delicate chin that formed the point of her heart-shaped face. I blinked, and I was back at the table again.

Recoiling, I gaped at Zelda. "What on earth was that?"

A human woman. See? Like I said, you all look ridiculous.

I rubbed my eyes. "I mean, what did you do? How did I see her photo?"

Her pointy teeth flashed in what might have been a smile, but it sent tingles down my spine. *I told you. I'm not just a cat.*

Mysterious comings and goings I could brush aside, but forcing an image into my brain? That bordered on mind control. It was frightening that such a little creature held so much power.

I drew back. "Can you read my mind?"

She gave her paw another lick. *Not if you keep feeding me more of that expensive tuna.*

My incredulous gaze shifted to Nolan, and I raised my eyebrows in question. With an exaggerated eye roll, he shook his head. Still, I'd be sleeping with one eye open.

Setting aside my future nightmares, I mentally summoned the picture of the mystery woman—this time, on my own. I didn't want Zelda having access to my brain again. "I've never seen that woman before."

"Neither have I," Nolan said. "And it's hard to tell if the photo is older or if it's a recent one edited with a filter to look aged."

Footsteps scuffed the hardwood as Dad shuffled into the kitchen. He caught sight of our strange group and hesitated. While he could only see me and Zelda, the chair Nolan occupied was positioned in such a way that it didn't look empty.

"Don't let me interrupt your, umm, meeting." He shivered before searching the cupboards for a snack.

I was too impatient to wait until he left before pressing on. "Did you find anything else?"

Nolan leaned in as though someone might overhear him. "We had a good look at his will."

Since he couldn't move objects, I pictured Zelda licking her pad before thumbing through the papers. A giggle bubbled in my throat, and I swallowed it back down. Nerves must have been getting to me. "How did you manage that?"

"Strangely, it was on his kitchen counter." He waved it off. "But get this. The person who inherits his estate is Grace Merriweather. Didn't you say Ingrid mentioned her?"

"Yes, she was Roman's old partner. Maybe it was his way of easing his guilt over cutting her out of the business, but Ingrid said Grace died some time ago."

"The date on the will is from years back, when she was alive, I assume. He probably had it out to update it."

Since Dad hadn't heard Nolan's response, he rounded the counter to come closer, but not too close. "Grace Merriweather? Cancer took her several years back. She died alone in a house on the edge of town. She was a quiet woman, kept to herself, so the community didn't know she needed help until it was too late. Such a shame." His focus dropped to the floor. "There were many people who would have been there for her." His mouth twisted as he resumed his snack hunt, and it was obvious he'd been one of those people.

In a tight-knit community like Hope, when push came to shove, people stood by one another. It was both a blessing and a curse since it meant everyone had their noses in your business. After Nolan had died, a lot of good people were there for me with kind words and hugs. At the time, though, it had felt as if more people were against me than supporting me. However, as I looked back, that might have been my survivor's guilt talking.

"I wonder why Roman hasn't changed his will after all these years," I mused. "But with Grace gone, his estate would go to her beneficiary. And since he's a successful, if shady, businessman, inheritance could be a motive." I turned back to my dad. "Did Grace have any children?"

He popped a chip into his mouth. "No family to speak of. She never married or had kids. Her parents passed a long time ago, and she was an only child. Maybe there were some distant relatives, but if there were, I've never heard tell of them." He held out the chip bag to me.

"No thanks," I said. "What happened to her house after she died?"

"It's still empty, as far as I know. There were probably a lot of medical bills and debt so, without a next of kin, the bank would have taken it over. They must have had trouble finding interested buyers. Island life is an acquired taste."

My shoulders sagged. "Then I guess the whole beneficiary lead is a dead end. Besides, unless the arsonist believed Roman was in the building at the time of the fire, it wasn't a direct attack on his life."

The woman with the salt-and-pepper braid sprang to mind, the one who'd asked if anyone was injured. Had she really been concerned, or had she secretly hoped it was Roman on that stretcher? I shook it off. If anyone had looked happy about the fire, it was Ingrid.

Facing my spies again, I focused on the other information they'd gathered. "You don't think that blond woman in the photo was Grace, do you?"

You mean the one with all the skin? Zelda asked helpfully.

Dad poured himself a bowl of chips. "Grace wasn't blond. Not the type to dye it either."

I recalled the youthfulness of the subject in the photo, her pale skin free of lines. "Not even when she was young?"

"Her parents were strict, always concerned about what

everyone in town thought. Even after their deaths, she remained reserved and kept to herself."

Slumping back in my chair, I groaned. "So tonight was pointless. We didn't uncover any clues to help Alice."

I wouldn't say pointless, Zelda said. *I expect my next can of tuna first thing in the morning.*

At least one of us had gotten something out of the ordeal.

Dad raised his bowl of chips in farewell. "I'll leave you to it then." With one last nervous glance around the room, he left the kitchen.

Zelda padded after him, presumably to get more pets. Or to scare the daylights out of him again.

I rubbed a hand over my face. "What now?" I asked, more to myself than Nolan.

He leaned forward anyway. "When I was visiting my family, I perused the guest list. Roman RSVP'd with a plus-one, meaning he'll probably bring one of his girlfriends along. It'll give you a chance to question them since you'll be there as a special cake server," he said like he didn't believe my cover story for a second.

Sighing, I figured I'd fess up to my plan. It wasn't as if he could stop me. "About that. I'm not going just to help Alice."

He chuckled. "I figured that. I know you want to be there to support Kinsley."

Ouch. While that was true, his innocent assumption made the rest of the truth harder to say. "And investigate your death. Like you pointed out the other day, I've made no headway in your case. The party will give me an opportunity to do some digging."

"Into whom?" Nolan squinted at me.

I cringed. "Your dad."

He shot to his feet. If he'd actually been sitting in the chair, the movement would have sent it flying back. "My dad had nothing to do with it."

"Even if that's true, I suspect he knows who did, like he's protecting someone."

His lips pulled into a tight line, and the vein on his forehead bulged—even though he had no blood pumping through it.

I rushed to explain. "Don't you think it's suspicious how he never pushed for the case to be solved? I mean, you were his son, the golden child. He should have gone to the ends of the earth to figure out what happened."

Nolan's nostrils flared, and he turned as if to leave, but he lingered in the doorway. When he said nothing, I continued.

"You know what the sheriff is like. He's a dog with a bone. He wouldn't have dropped the case unless he was certain it was an accident. Not unless the actual power, the town's mayor, put pressure on him."

Jaw working, he was quiet for a few moments. "I… I hadn't thought about it like that. I remember very little from that time. The first few years were all a blur of emotions and old memories driving me." Shoving his hands into his pockets, he dropped his gaze to the floor. "But still. This is my dad we're talking about. I don't appreciate you investigating him like he's some criminal."

"You asked me to solve your murder. Unless you have a better idea, this is my only lead."

He looked prepared to argue, but I didn't give him the chance. Instead, I shut off the kitchen light and stomped up to bed. I'd need my sleep for the next day if I was to face an engagement party at the same place I'd had my fateful rehearsal dinner.

CHAPTER THIRTEEN

As the groom-to-be regaled the party guests with tales of his endless love for Kinsley, he was every bit the charmer I'd expected. Lorenzo could have read an insurance brochure aloud in his thick Italian accent and still held the audience spellbound. It didn't hurt that his backdrop was one of the best views on the island.

The reception was being held at The Lodge, a rustic name for the modern architectural feat on the side of the mountain range locals referred to as Sleeping Beauty. It perched on a knoll most argued was the beauty's breast. Or was it her wrist? Either way, while floor-to-ceiling windows provided a breath-taking view, it was still just a short hike from downtown. Other-wise, those residents without wheels—as in most of them—wouldn't have been able to get there.

"Everyone must be curious about how we met. It's a funny story." Lorenzo chuckled, causing everyone else to do the same as though he were their puppeteer. "I was in Roma, and the wine had just been poured…"

Alice leaned on our cake table at the back of the room. "I hope my next meet-cute involves drinking wine in Italy with a man like that." She nudged me with an elbow. "But look who I'm talking to. You just got back from there."

"I'm sure my experiences were far different from Kinsley's." Not to mention, I hadn't been open to dating. Then again, I might have been tempted by a man as charming as Lorenzo, with his tailored suit, amiable smile, and perfectly swooped hair.

As he spoke on stage about his upcoming nuptials, I thought back to mine—or, rather, the night before mine were supposed to happen. It was impossible not to. Same venue, many of the same guests, and my fiancé in the audience, still wearing the same suit. There was one striking difference, though. At our rehearsal dinner, Mr. and Mrs. Abernathy had moped and drunk as if it were their last meal, while tonight, they hung on Lorenzo's every word and laughed in all the right places. And why not? He was cut from the same cloth as they were, and they couldn't be happier. Meanwhile, as far as a daughter-in-law went, I'd resembled a patchwork quilt.

The microphone made the rounds until Kinsley held it in her dainty hands, the resized ring sparkling on her finger. "Well, I think we've had enough speeches for one night. You're probably eyeing that gorgeous cake in the back, created by Batch of the Day. Please eat, dance, and enjoy yourselves."

As soon as the chandeliers dimmed, eager guests filtered our way. Alice leaped into action, cutting fresh slices of the ivory cake adorned with golden fondant leaves and delicate sugar flowers.

We looked like real pros in our matching pink-and-black polka-dot tops. When I'd given her the shirts, as expected, she'd argued. However, after trying one on, she hugged me and insisted I wear one during the party to match her. I was glad I had. It helped me fade into the background, just another staff member, while I eavesdropped on guests who came to the table for a slice.

Nolan lingered nearby. I knew he resented my ulterior

motive for being there, but he needn't have worried. I could barely keep up with demand, let alone listen in on guests' conversations or interrogate his mother when she approached for a slice of cake. Not that she'd even deign to discuss the weather with me. The only acknowledgment I received from her was a contemptuous curl of her lip as she took a plate.

While I'd come to gather intel on Nolan's murder, many of the key players in my other investigation also came up to the table, including Milton, Ingrid, and Pepper. If my queries into Mr. Abernathy turned up nothing, at least I might solve Alice's case.

The rush died down, and people mingled over cocktails or spun around the dance floor to music performed by an orchestra that the Abernathys had flown in from who knows where. But Alice was far from ready to call it a night. Excited about her first gig, she was on a mission to give everyone a sugar rush and pounced on any guest who neared the table.

At one point, Jason and Sheriff Reed passed by. They were attached at the hip even when off duty, which made it even stranger to see them in suits and not their uniforms.

Alice presented a plate of cake. "Care for a slice, Sheriff?"

Reed raised a palm. "It looks delicious, but I try to stay away from the stuff. I'm diabetic."

She pulled the plate away like she'd aimed a loaded gun at him. "Oh, that's right. Sorry. How about you, Jason?"

"None for me either. I'm saving the calories for a drink tonight." He patted his midsection, even though I suspected a six-pack hid beneath his suit.

Thankfully, I didn't share his enthusiasm for a strict dietary regimen. I was eager to dig into the extra tier Alice had dropped off for my dad and me. It was waiting at home in the fridge.

As the two officers wandered off, Alice's posture wilted. I deflated too; it was hard to eavesdrop with no one around.

Scanning the room, I spotted Pepper's red chiffon dress fluttering toward the restrooms.

Earlier that day, I'd tried once more to stop by Mew to You, only to find a Spring Sale sign out front and a slew of deal seekers inside. Now, this was my best opportunity to get the woman alone.

"I'll be right back," I told Alice before beelining it across the dance floor.

Nolan followed close behind. I ignored him and tried to catch snippets of conversations as I passed clusters of guests. While I picked up on the odd scathing remark aimed at the Abernathys, it mostly centered on dinner's questionable shellfish and the ostentatious decor.

Excusing my way through a group caught in a heated sports debate, I pretended not to hear the argument between a couple by the snack table. *Strange.* It seemed early for the party to be getting so rowdy. Then again, there was an open bar.

The clamor dimmed as I slipped into the corridor to the restrooms. In the quiet, heels clicked loudly behind me. The sounds echoed down the long hall like little pops of gunfire. Curiously, I turned just as Nolan called out.

"Mother, no!"

I glimpsed Christine Abernathy's haughty face twist with fury a second before she gripped my upper arm. With the skirts of her elegant dress clutched in one fist, she dragged me out of sight.

Her long gel nails dug into my skin. "You don't deserve to be here."

Scowling, I tried to yank my arm away. Okay, she hated me. Memo received. So I hadn't been invited, but did she despise me so much that I couldn't even work at the event? "I-I'm here to serve cake."

"Not here. I mean, you don't deserve to be alive. Nolan's dead because of you." She spoke between clenched teeth. "It should have been you. Not him."

Nolan reached out as though to pull the woman off me, but his arms fell through her. "Mother, how could you say that?"

Her words stung. They were too close to the truth that had lived in my heart since that terrible night. She didn't need to remind me he wouldn't have been in that car, upset and distracted as he navigated the winding road, if it hadn't been for me. Why had I deserved to live while Nolan hadn't?

Christine's nostrils flared like she wasn't there to vent about my survival but to remedy it. But why now? During her daughter's special evening?

Her behavior felt so out of place, so sudden, that I couldn't believe it was real. However, the fear rippling down my spine told me it was very real. Although I'd come for answers, something urged me to get out of there.

Pulling away, I tore out of her grasp and raced down the hall. I needed to be among the other guests, witnesses. Before I made it to the ballroom, she caught up and whipped me around to face her.

"You don't get off that easy. Nolan didn't." Despite the hatred in her eyes, tears streamed past her fake eyelashes. "He was the good one, the kind and generous one, the one who brought people together. And you're nothing but trouble."

Nolan's mouth hung open. He looked ready to reach out to her again, but I wasn't sure if he meant to save me or hug his brokenhearted mother.

While I didn't disagree with her, I repeated the mantra I'd told myself a hundred times in the hopes I'd one day believe it. "It wasn't my fault. I was the passenger. I almost died too."

"You stupid girl," she hissed, veneered teeth bared. "How do you think you survived and he didn't? His powers were protective. He could have used his magic to save himself, but instead, here you are."

I wanted to pretend I didn't know what she was talking about. Magic? That was only in fairy tales. But I was too shocked. My breath whooshed out of me like she'd kicked me in the stomach.

"What? No. That can't be true." I wasn't trying to run anymore. Not because I'd finally found some answers but because my legs wouldn't work.

"He died so you could live." Her gaze scraped over me. "What a waste."

My legs finally gave out, and I sank to the floor in front of the irate woman. I turned to Nolan, who looked down on me with what could only be described as pity. A dead man was pitying me.

"Tell me it's not true," I begged him.

With a grimace, he shoved his hands into his pockets and stared at his shoes.

Christine assumed I was speaking to her. "If only."

As the truth seeped in, an old wound ripped open inside me, making room for this new layer of guilt.

My survival had come at the expense of my fiancé's life.

CHAPTER FOURTEEN

I scrambled to my feet and ran from Christine Abernathy. Having successfully wounded me, she let me go. I burst through Nolan's ethereal form, dispersing it in a cloud of smoke, and raced for the restroom—the one place he was too much of a gentleman to follow. After turning on the taps, I splashed cold water onto my face as though I could wash away the truth. Nolan had died because of me.

As I dabbed my skin dry with a hand towel—no unsophisticated paper towels for the Abernathys—I stared at my reflection, trying to process this new bombshell. But I couldn't. Not yet. My emotions felt too raw to sort through in such a public space, surrounded by strangers, Nolan's family, and an arsonist I'd yet to uncover.

A stall door squeaked open behind me. Pepper stepped out, and we locked eyes in the mirror's reflection. I'd forgotten she was the reason I'd headed for the restroom in the first place.

She gave me a sympathetic look. "Are you all right, dear?"

All right? No. I definitely wasn't, but I attempted to rearrange my panic-stricken features.

Get it together, Vi.

I finished drying my face and tossed the towel into the basket. "I'm fine. It was getting warm in there, and I needed to cool myself down."

She washed her hands. "You don't have to pretend with me. This isn't my crowd either. I'm not even sure why I'm here."

One reason came to mind: Roman. Was she his date? I hadn't seen them together earlier when Pepper grabbed a slice of cake.

"Did you come here with someone?" I asked.

She pulled out her ruby-red lipstick to freshen up but then threw it back into her purse, unused. "No. He's here with someone else, but that's nothing new. We're not in a committed relationship or anything."

Pepper had tamed her normally frizzy hair into an updo, and her red dress hugged her ample curves as only an expensive label could, probably a lucky find from her shop. Had she dressed to the nines hoping to impress Roman?

"You don't seem thrilled about that arrangement," I said.

"It used to suit me fine, since I swore never to remarry. It's just me and my daughter, and I can't imagine bringing anyone else into our world. Especially not a man like Roman." She pressed her fingers to her lips. "Oops. I suppose I let the cat out of the bag."

Her frankness surprised me. Maybe she felt at ease because she'd caught me having a moment. "If it makes you feel any better, I'd already heard." Since I didn't want to reveal my source, I shrugged. "Small-town life."

"Isn't that the truth?" Her sigh carried a hint of a laugh. "Roman isn't so bad. He makes me feel special when we're together. At least, I believed I was special. Now, he's found yet another woman. But like you said, small-town life. It leads to a shallow dating pool."

I recalled how Milton had been admiring her. That pool was probably deeper than she realized. "I don't know. There are some decent bachelors out there. Take Milton Curry, for example."

"Milton?" Her eyelashes fluttered in surprise. "Don't get me wrong. The man's a catch. For one, he's great with kids. He volunteers for the children's activity table at all the festivals. And he'd make a great husband. You can always tell by the way a man treats his mother, and he treated his like a queen." She pursed her lips thoughtfully. "But while he's friendly to everyone, he seems… distant. Off the market, you know? He got his heart broken once and never recovered."

Was she referring to the same woman Milton's mother had harassed him about, the one Roman had stolen from him? While it sounded like a long time ago, he might have been brokenhearted enough to still want revenge. Time could heal all wounds, but it could also make them fester.

"I think it makes him sound romantic," I said. "Do you know who the woman was?"

Pepper's vintage earrings caught the light as she shook her head. "No. He's pretty secretive. Like I said, distant."

I tried not to let my disappointment show. Perhaps the only people alive—and dead—who'd know the old love's identity were Roman, Milton, and Mrs. Curry.

The restroom door swung open, ending my chance to get more info out of Pepper. As I assessed the newcomer sashaying toward us in a slinky black dress, I recognized her from past Abernathy soirees. The willowy blond woman was a successful real estate agent from Serenity. Elaine something.

Fists balled, she stormed up to Pepper. "Can you believe he brought her here? The nerve of him, flaunting his shiny new toy in front of our faces." She jolted, as though just realizing I was standing there. "Hello." She took in my polka-dotted shirt. "I loved the cake. Compliments to the baker."

"Elaine, this is Violet," Pepper said. "I was confiding in her about our love triangle. She's an excellent listener."

It felt like the comment was aimed at me, a subtle request to keep it under wraps. I nodded.

Elaine pressed a palm to her chest. "You told her about Roman? About me?"

Pepper held up a hand. "To be fair, I let it slip about my dating life. It was poor timing that spilled your own secret when you came storming in here."

"Wait," I interrupted, my sluggish mind only now catching up to the new breakthrough. "You know you're both dating the same man, and you don't have it in for each other?" My theory about one of them wanting revenge on Roman wasn't looking too good.

Pepper winked at the other woman. "It's better to have an ally than an enemy. We've formed a close friendship."

"In fact," Elaine added, "it's the only positive thing that came from dating Roman. At least, I assume it's over. We've barely heard from him in the last week. It's that new pastry chef. She's got that pig wrapped around her little finger. I can't believe he brought her tonight."

Neither could I. A third woman and his new employee, of all people? However, it struck me as harsh to call someone she was dating a pig, especially when she'd acted so breezy about sharing him. Did she care more than she was letting on?

She paced, vibrating with the same energy as when she'd burst into the restroom. "You know what? I say we go introduce ourselves to the new girl. Set her straight about how things work around here."

Pepper tucked her purse under her arm like she was preparing for battle. "I'm more interested in giving Roman a piece of my mind. I've had enough of these games." She turned to me. "Our talk has helped me come to my senses. Thank you."

I jerked back. That had escalated quickly. "I didn't mean to—"

But they were already shoving open the restroom door to return to the party.

Stunned, I watched them go. All the power to them, but I didn't want any blame for what was about to happen.

Both concerned and curious, I nearly followed them but then reconsidered. This was one time I should stay away from trouble, especially since I'd spurred it on somehow. Plus, I was tired of snooping for one night. I'd already learned more about Nolan's death than I'd been prepared for.

As I headed back to rejoin Alice, I attempted to block out the conversations around me, but they still found their way to my ears. Many of the guests were speaking loudly. In fact, they were downright yelling at each other, hurling insults and scathing retorts over the music.

I eyed the main table, where Kinsley covered her face with a napkin while she sobbed. Lorenzo rubbed her back while her mother stood a ways off, posture as stiff as her smile. When Christine's sweeping gaze found mine, her eyes narrowed into slits. I veered in the opposite direction.

A meaty *thwack* sounded nearby. I leaped out of the way just as a man in a torn dress shirt tumbled to the floor. He wiped blood from the corner of his mouth then lurched to his feet and charged another guest.

A fistfight? This was supposed to be a joyful celebration. What were they serving at that open bar?

Wondering if Alice and I should call it a night, I rushed back to the cake table. My heart lurched as I saw another fight brewing, this time between Roman and Alice. Colette stood a few feet away from her alleged date, appearing thoroughly bored by the confrontation.

Chest puffed up, Roman gestured to the remaining plates of cake. "Can't seem to give the stuff away, huh? They should have left the baking to the real professionals."

A flush crept over Alice's fair cheeks and neck, blossoming

across her chest. The plate in her hands shook like she was fighting the desire to chuck the cake at him.

I rushed to take over, but whether it was to serve him or smash the cake in his egotistical face myself was up in the air. Alice shot me a grateful look and stepped aside to gather herself.

Ignoring Roman, I plastered on a grin and faced Colette. "Would you like a slice?"

Her lip curled as if I'd offered her a slug, but she took a plate from the table anyway. "Why not? It will allow me to check out the competition." Her cheek dimpled at the reference to our last meeting, and she took a delicate bite. "It is quite good."

"Good?" Roman's guffaw boomed, drowning out the music. "Who needs to settle for good when we have mag-nee-feek?" He butchered the word with his poor attempt at a French accent. Throwing a heavy arm around Colette, he sloshed his drink onto her bare shoulder. Always the charmer.

She stiffened, too polite to outright recoil. She couldn't possibly be interested. Then again, she was too new in town to have received an invitation to the party. That must have meant Elaine was right and she was his plus-one.

Colette took the plate Alice was still holding and thrust it at him. "Roman, do not torture the poor girl. Has she not been through enough this week? I have had the cake, and it tastes good. Now, stop being so rude and eat it already."

I flinched at her sharp tone. Maybe the date wasn't going so well. Against my will, I liked the woman despite the trouble her arrival had caused for Alice.

Roman reluctantly took the plate. However, before he even had a bite, Pepper stomped up to him and snatched it away.

She glared at the French woman. "I can give this to him, thank you very much. You've monopolized him enough for one night, and we have things to discuss."

While Pepper wasn't one to hide her emotions, it usually

meant you'd catch her getting misty-eyed or laughing with abandon. The contempt wrinkling her nose was a new look for the woman.

Hindered by her form-fitting dress, Elaine finally caught up. She aimed a sneer at Colette before wrenching the plate away from Pepper. "He doesn't enjoy cake. You'd know that if you really understood him like I do."

The two friends bickered, broadcasting their love triangle to anyone within earshot. Soon, they drew a crowd, and the other guests shouted support for one side or the other as though this were a wrestling match and not an engagement party. Ingrid was the loudest of them, whistling and calling for blood—Roman's, surprise, surprise. Even Milton was among them, in Pepper's corner.

Alice and I exchanged a shocked look. What was going on?

Mayor Abernathy's combed-back hair bobbed above the crowd as he moved from guest to guest, patting backs congenially. His smooth chuckle drifted through the air as he pretended this was all just a misunderstanding. Did he think he could charm people into submission? Who would he even start with? Were Pepper and Elaine upset at Roman, Colette, or each other?

If the soap opera–level drama shocked the French woman, she didn't show it. "Roman, do you know these women?"

His Adam's apple bobbed. "Yeah, they're… umm, friends."

Pepper bristled. "Friends? Is that all?" But she didn't give him a chance to respond. "You know what? Don't even bother, because we're through. I'm tired of letting you have your cake and eat it too." She grabbed the plate from Elaine and shoved it against his belly.

He took the treat and stared blankly at it. This was the first time I'd ever seen the man at a loss for words. As the women continued to argue, he gave a "whatever" shrug and picked up the fork. He shoveled the cake into his mouth as if it were a bag of popcorn and he was enjoying the show.

Elaine jabbed a manicured finger at Pepper. "You never loved him like I did."

"Love?" Pepper snickered. "Is that what it is? You have a funny way of showing it."

And back and forth it went.

Roman was nearly done with his slice when the fork froze halfway to his mouth. Perhaps one of their comments had hit a nerve. His expression twisted. With heartbreak? Regret? Maybe he had genuine feelings for these women after all.

Then the large man swayed like a tree in the wind before he fell back, crashing onto the table.

Alice and I jumped back as it collapsed beneath his weight. Cake launched into the air, splattering the surrounding guests. They cried out, wiping icing from their hair and expensive outfits.

A woman screamed. It was Elaine. She pointed at Roman with one hand over her mouth as if she was going to be sick. He writhed on the parquet floor, spittle flying from his mouth between gasps of air. Was he choking?

Pepper rushed forward. "Someone call an ambulance!"

She knelt beside him. In his desperate flailing, he hit her in the face with a loud *whack*.

She reeled back, massaging her cheek, and Elaine helped her to her feet. They clung to each other, their earlier fight forgotten. Neither of them tried to approach the struggling man again, and Colette appeared carved out of marble. In fact, no one seemed to know quite what to do.

Roman searched the guests' shocked expressions, bulging eyes begging for help. His face darkened from red to purple. He tugged on his tie, frantically tearing open his shirt in a desperate fight for air. After a few futile gasps, he grew still.

While I stared at him, I distantly felt Alice's nails digging into my arm. Everyone else had moved back to give Roman space. I was now the closest to him. When no one else moved, I stepped over the table.

Careful to avoid the broken plates, I crouched next to him and pressed my fingers to his neck. His skin was slick with sweat, and my hands shook as I searched for his pulse. I felt nothing.

"He's dead."

CHAPTER FIFTEEN

Roman's lifeless eyes stared at me, his mouth parted as if poised to tell me a secret. I had to do something. But what? My brain flitted from one thought to another until it finally landed on a useful idea: chest compressions.

I leaned over his still body, linked my fingers, and pumped. It was more difficult than I'd expected. Was it even working? The sightless brown orbs looking back at me seemed to say, "Not even a little."

Someone squeezed my shoulder. Sheriff Reed. For the first time since I could remember, his expression wasn't guarded as he looked at me but reassuring.

He knelt beside me and placed his hands over mine on Roman's chest. "It's okay. I've got this."

I didn't argue and moved away to join the other guests. As the sheriff bounced up and down, trying to save Roman, I thought I must be in shock because my vision blurred. Only not everything turned hazy. Just Roman's body.

With each compression, a sort of fog was forced out of him, from his mouth, his nose, his every pore. I watched with growing alarm and observed the other guests, wondering if they saw it too. Then the strange vapor condensed, taking on a human form, and I understood.

Oh, joy. Roman was a ghost.

His spirit blinked and surveyed the room, brow furrowing as he took in the sea of shocked faces. When his focus landed on the body at his feet, his eyes widened. He stumbled back in surprise, right through Pepper and Elaine, who were still hugging each other and staring at their dead boyfriend.

After a shocked moment, he addressed the two women, mouth moving silently. Naturally, they didn't respond. Not used to being ignored, he planted himself in front of Pepper and reached out to grab her. However, his hands passed straight through her. Pepper shuddered but otherwise didn't react. His mouth hung open while he examined his hands like he didn't recognize them.

Roman's ghost began to pace, pleading with the other partygoers. His attempts to elicit a response from them quickly escalated into frustration and yelling. It reminded me of Nolan's disorientation when he'd first died, the way he'd tried so desperately to be heard, to be seen. I kept my attention averted, afraid even a hint of acknowledgment would reveal my powers to him and he'd zero in on me.

"Did he choke?" a man nearby asked, though no one seemed to have an answer.

A woman in a sapphire dress dabbed at the tears forming in her eyes with a napkin. "It must have been a heart attack."

As tactful as ever, Ingrid cackled. "That's karma for you."

Roman's icy stare bored into the woman as his lips shaped an expletive clear enough to read. His look was so cold, I almost expected her to shiver beneath it.

"That was no heart attack," someone with a thick Italian accent exclaimed. "I think he was poisoned."

"Poisoned?!" an elderly woman screeched. "What did he eat?"

A server pointed at the broken table. "The cake. I definitely saw him eating the cake before he died."

Roman spun to study the heap of icing and crumbs on the floor before rounding on Alice, who stood frozen, watching the scene in stunned silence. Nostrils flaring, he stalked toward her. His form seemed to blur, shaking with barely contained rage. I stepped forward but held back, reminding myself there was nothing he could do to her. At least, I hoped so.

Meanwhile, the living guests were starting to come to the same conclusion as Roman, and while no one began lighting torches, they shot Alice accusatory glances.

She backed away, shaking her head. "Th-The cake isn't poisoned, I swear." Her voice squeaked out. "I would never do something like that." Tears spilled down her cheeks before she turned and ran.

A few guests pursued her, but Jason blocked their path. "Whoa, let's keep a level head. Everyone, please move to the other side of the room and give the sheriff some space."

"Jason." Reed sounded out of breath, but his chest compressions never faltered. "Call in backup from Serenity if they can spare anyone. And make sure no one leaves."

The response from the crowd was a few muttered arguments, but no one ignored the order. Yet.

There was something in the air tonight. Even mild-mannered Milton was scowling and shooting daggers around the room. Jason dragged a hand through his styled hair as he took in the rowdy guests. When everyone was a potential threat, where did you start?

I'd expected Roman to follow on Alice's heels, but instead, he turned back to his body. His shoulders sank as though they were suddenly too heavy, and he crossed over to the women he'd been dating. He paused before Pepper first, then Elaine, his mouth forming words I was glad I couldn't hear. When he reached Colette, his features crumpled. Despite how briefly he'd known her, she seemed to be the biggest regret of his tangled dating life. He'd obviously had high hopes for this date.

Reluctantly, Roman turned and headed in the direction Alice had gone. My heart crawled its way up my throat with worry. While he shouldn't have been able to harm Alice, what did I really know about the dead?

I recalled my last ghost, how in a blind rage, he'd been able to physically weigh down his killer until he nearly drowned. Roman had been furious enough when he thought Alice was responsible for the bakery fire. Now, if he blamed her for his death, what might he be capable of?

Not willing to find out, I followed him, weaving through the throng of people that resembled a mob. By the time I'd pushed my way to the other side of the room, Roman was slipping through the exit. Maybe Alice had gone outside for fresh air, so I ran after him.

The doors flew open at my forceful push, and I burst into the night. The wail of an approaching ambulance grew louder as it headed for The Lodge. I scanned the manicured grounds illuminated by the chandeliers' light pouring out through the wall of windows. Standing in its glow, a semitransparent Roman gazed back inside, longing etched into his face. Whether it was for his lost loves or lost life, I couldn't be sure.

I considered making my powers known to him, if only to talk him down a little. However, his earlier anger seemed to have subsided. His chest rose and fell in a sigh before he turned away. In a puff of smoke, he disappeared as suddenly as if he'd stepped through a door and slammed it shut behind him.

I flinched. I guessed that was the end of Roman Fedoro.

If the man had been bothered by his strange death or haunted by guilt over how he'd treated people, it seemed he hadn't been concerned enough to stick around and dwell on it. Or else that wasn't what being a ghost was about. Perhaps those who lingered did so because they were tethered to something in this world, and Roman had spent his life ensuring nothing tied him down. Whether he'd have to face his regrets on the other side or not, I was just relieved I wouldn't be the one to help him do it.

When the sirens shut off, plunging the night into silence, I called into the darkness beyond the building's glow. "Alice? Are you out here?"

No answer. She'd probably run to the restroom, but I wasn't ready to go back inside. Needing to gather my thoughts, I followed the paving-stone path that snaked across the lawn until the walkway ended abruptly at the edge of the forest. I paused and inhaled deeply. The cool air cleared my head, and the scent of damp soil grounded me.

Embraced in solitude, it was easy to sense the presence behind me. I knew it was Nolan. Bracing myself, I swung around to face him. He looked solid in the near dark, as if he were really standing there. A sense of déjà vu hit me, transporting me back to the night of the accident. Only now did I notice I'd gravitated to the same spot I'd fled to after the argument with his father.

Like that night, I had so many questions whirling through my mind. How had Nolan saved me? Why hadn't he told me the truth since I'd returned?

I opened my mouth to ask, but grass swished nearby. Someone was coming toward me, and fast. My questions would have to wait.

My muscles tensed, and I squinted against the building's bright lights. Considering how enraged everyone was, my instincts screamed at me to run. However, as the stalking figure approached, I recognized his gait and the familiar contours of his silhouette.

I relaxed. "Max?"

"Why did you leave?" he demanded, not slowing his pace.

I frowned at the anger in his voice. "I needed some air."

He stopped a foot away, looming over me. "I mean, why did you leave Charm Island? Why did you cut me out of your life? I lost Nolan too. We could have been there for each other." He cringed. "Was it because of what I said that night?"

The hurt and longing in Max's expression tugged at something deep inside me, something I was having a harder time pushing back down lately. I reached out, yearning to touch him.

Nolan shifted closer. "What is he talking about?"

Remembering myself, I snatched my hand back. While Max deserved an answer, I couldn't give it to him now. His confession of love for me the night before the wedding wasn't something my fiancé had known about in life. I certainly wouldn't tell him now that I knew he'd died for my sake.

"Not now," I told Max, sweeping past him.

He grabbed my arm. "When? It's been five years. I need… closure." He grimaced as though he'd swallowed a fishing hook.

The heat in his voice surprised me because he'd been nothing but lukewarm since my return. "Where is this coming from all of a sudden?" Maybe it was thanks to whatever was affecting all the other guests.

His nostrils flared, and I braced myself for his next words. Thankfully, footsteps approached, and we both turned to the sound. A flashlight flicked on, the blinding beam aimed at Max's face.

"Everything okay here?" It was Jason.

Max dropped my arm to shield his eyes. "We're fine, thanks. This is a private matter."

The deputy came closer. "I don't think she wants to talk to you."

As Max sized him up, fists clenched at his sides, the light reflected in his eyes like an animal's. It took me back to the last time his anger had flared in front of me. It couldn't be my imagination, not on two different occasions.

He jerked his head back and forth, resembling a dog flinging off water. When he looked at me once more, his face was clear of emotion. He was a stranger to me again. This was the standoffish Max I'd gotten used to since my return.

"Sorry," he said. "I don't know why I said any of that. I have to go."

He stormed off, clipping Jason's shoulder as he left. Nolan gave me a curious glance before he followed his friend. It took everything I had not to follow my fiancé and beg him to stay in case he heard something I didn't want him to.

Bewildered, I stared after Max. Was tonight the night to air dirty laundry? Something was wrong, and since it had affected so many of the guests, an open bar or bad shellfish couldn't explain it. The situation seemed almost… paranormal. Did I have something to do with it? Anything was possible since I didn't understand the extent of my powers yet.

And whose fault is that? an annoying inner voice asked.

Jason drew closer. "Are you okay?"

I pressed a hand to my forehead. "Just overwhelmed by everything that's happened tonight."

"As your friend, if you want to talk about it, I'm here for you." He gave my arm a squeeze before pulling away. "But as a deputy, I have to switch roles and question you. I wish it could wait, but we need to clear people out of here. Things are quickly getting out of hand."

"Of course." How could I argue? There was a dead body, and once again, I'd been closest to it.

I noticed Jason was acting his normal self, so the surge of anger that had ripped through the party hadn't affected everyone. Reed had also kept his wits about him, which was a relief; the sheriff and his deputy were the two people I knew who had guns.

Jason drew out his phone and started a voice recording. "You were close to Roman when he collapsed. Can you describe the events leading up to that?"

While I almost skipped my chat with Elaine and Pepper, their love triangle was no longer a secret. Plus, while they'd claimed to be happy to share one man, their actions after leaving the restroom told another story, so I began there.

"It sounds as though you'd been away from Alice for a while," he said. "You didn't see her dish up Roman's piece of cake?"

"She cut slices ahead of time so they'd be ready to go." I narrowed my eyes. "What are you getting at? Do you really believe someone poisoned him?" Realization struck me, and I clapped a hand over my mouth. "You think Alice did."

His handsome features stiffened. "Until we get the autopsy results back—"

I waved off his formal response. "This is Alice we're talking about. She's not capable of murder. Roman could have died of natural causes. A heart attack maybe."

Jason paused the recording. "I don't want to see Alice behind bars any more than you do, but things aren't looking good for her. First the fire and Caitlin, and now, this."

"How do you know Caitlin didn't set the fire?"

"The reports came back," he said. "We're pretty certain."

"How certain?" I pressed.

He checked our surroundings, but we were alone. "There was no smoke in her lungs or elevated levels of carbon monoxide in her blood. She was dead before the fire even started. Her pockets were full of bills, and the store's safe was empty." He shrugged. "We think she was only there to rob Roman."

This new tidbit of knowledge clicked something into place like a puzzle piece. When Caitlin's ghost had been muttering to herself, I must have misheard. She wasn't saying, *I take it back.* She was begging someone, possibly Roman, to *Take it back.* As in the money. The guilt preventing her from moving on hadn't been about the fire at all. I wondered if her plea to *Tell them I'm sorry* had been meant for her parents.

"Did you return the money to the store?" I asked.

Jason gave me a strange look, probably wondering why, out

of all the questions I could have asked, I'd chosen that one. "Yeah. That part of the case was cut and dried, so we gave it back to Roman. Why?"

"It doesn't matter." But it did matter for Caitlin. If the stolen money had been holding her back, returning it might have inadvertently resolved her unfinished business and released her spirit. That could be why Nolan and I hadn't found her. While that meant I could no longer question her, I hoped she'd moved on to a better place.

Now that she was off the list of suspects, I searched for a new angle. "Do you think the real arsonist was in on the robbery with Caitlin? Maybe they fought over it and things turned violent."

Jason shifted from foot to foot. "Look. I've already told you too much."

"Please." I locked gazes with him. "I can help. You want to clear Alice's name, don't you?"

He shook his head but relented anyway. "We think the two crimes are unrelated. Likely, Caitlin chose the wrong time to hit the store and caught the arsonist red-handed. So they strangled her with kitchen twine."

I drew in a sharp breath. I'd thought the rope around her neck was a braided necklace of sorts, but the poor girl had been strangled. How awful.

My lip curled with disgust at what Jason was suggesting. "If Alice is your prime suspect in all of this, that means you think she, your own cousin, killed Caitlin."

"You know I love her like a sister, but unless you can give me something else to go on, I can't help her. So please, Vi. Help me help Alice."

His expression was so pained and sincere that it dissolved my fight. He was right; arguing about her innocence wouldn't do any good. I had to find the actual guilty party.

"I left the cake table a while before the incident. When I came back, the plate was in Alice's hands, ready to be served.

She wasn't the only one who handled it before Roman ate it, though. All three women he was dating touched it at one point."

"Did you see any of them do anything to it?"

"No. I was too wrapped up in their fight, and the crowd they'd drawn blocked my view."

As I replayed the scene in my mind, I remembered Milton had been there too. While I didn't want to believe him capable of poisoning the cake, he had seemed uncharacteristically aggressive tonight—along with everyone else. And Ingrid's threat to Roman only hours before the fire rang in my ears. *You're a dead man.* However, I didn't want to throw suspicion on them just because they were in a bad mood and in the vicinity. I had no evidence they'd done anything. If my investigation revealed more, I'd come forward.

"Were you with Alice when she baked the cake?" Jason asked.

"No. I helped her load it and transport it after. But the entire cake wasn't poisoned or else we'd have more dead bodies in there."

"Are you sure about that?" He studied the venue then faced me again as though debating whether to say more. "Something is affecting all the guests. A reaction to an ingredient Roman was sensitive to, or a poison that had built up in his system over time. Like I said, forensics will tell us more."

I had to admit, he'd made a good point. And as Roman's long-suffering employee, Alice would have had the means to poison him over an extended period. While I didn't believe for a second that she'd done anything, if I was being objective, she was the most likely suspect.

The breath I released shifted the hair lying across my forehead. "Alice is in trouble, isn't she?"

Jason's attention flicked to something behind me. "Yes, she is."

I followed his gaze to the parking lot and spotted Sheriff

Reed escorting Alice to his SUV. Before Jason could stop me, I raced in their direction. I got there just as the back door shut with Alice inside.

"This isn't right," I told Reed. "You can't arrest her without more evidence." I had no idea if that was true. If I was going to make a habit out of solving crimes, I needed to watch more detective shows.

Reed yanked off his tie as if fed up with the suit. "I'm not arresting her, Miss Woods. It's for her own safety. The crowd is agitated, and they're pointing fingers at her." He tossed Jason the keys. "I've already questioned her. I figured it would be better if you took her home."

"Yes, sir." Jason nodded before hopping behind the wheel.

I blinked, my fury derailed, and took in our surroundings. Guests poured out of the building, some in pursuit of the action and a few others to brawl. Reed was right. Things had escalated. People clustered around the vehicle, and I had the urge to bang on the hood and yell at Jason, "Drive!"

As I studied the mob, one face stuck out. Not just because she was familiar but because I'd never seen her until the day all the trouble had started. It was the older woman with the long salt-and-pepper braid who'd been there during Alice's firing. Then, I'd spoken with her after the fire. Now, here she was again on the heels of Roman's sudden death.

I wanted to point her out to Reed. Better yet, I wished Nolan would return so I could ask him to tail her, but I was probably being paranoid. She might have been new to town. Also, she wasn't acting riotous like the other guests. Instead, she looked heartbroken. Another one of Roman's lovers, perhaps?

Jason turned over the cruiser's engine and chirped the siren. My heart leaped at the sound, and I spun away from the woman. When I glanced back to search for her, she'd disappeared into the swarming crowd.

Before the SUV pulled away, I knocked on the rear door's window. "Alice?"

She didn't look at me. Face buried in her palms, she continued to sob.

Because I could hear her cry, I knew she'd hear me, so I said, "Everything will be okay. I promise."

But it was hard to sound convincing, because I wasn't sure how it would be.

CHAPTER SIXTEEN

The early-morning sun peeked through my window, dragging me from a too-short and fitful sleep. I turned over, hoping to squeeze a few more minutes out of the night. But when I settled back onto my pillow, it felt like an ice cube was resting against my nose.

My eyes flicked open. From the other side of my double bed, Nolan stared back at me. He was positioned as though we'd been spooning before I'd rolled over.

"What the…" I reared back and kicked off the covers.

A lump beneath the blanket stirred, and Zelda's muffled voice drifted out. *Hey! Some people are trying to sleep around here.*

Claustrophobia gripped me. I scrambled out of bed and threw on my housecoat. "What do you think you're doing?"

Zelda poked her head out. *I'm doing gymnastics. What does it look like? Keep it down, would you?*

"Not you," I hissed, remembering Dad was still asleep.

Lying on his side, Nolan propped his head on one fist. "I thought you'd want some company after last night."

"I don't need a ghost and a cat in my bed." *Well, a cat would be nice*, I conceded to myself. *But not this one.* "What happened to our deal? I told you I'd solve your murder, but you were supposed to give me space. This," I gestured at my bed, "is the opposite of space."

I shoved my feet into my fuzzy slippers, stormed from my bedroom, and descended the stairs. The grandfather clock said it was six a.m., still too early to call Alice. She was usually an early riser, but I'd received her last text message after one in the morning, so I doubted she'd be up yet. I'd begged her to sleep over at my place so she wouldn't be alone, but she'd claimed to be fine. Yes, I got the hypocrisy since I'd yelled at Nolan for his impromptu sleepover, but she would have had her own bed.

Ignoring what I'd just said about space, Nolan followed me into the kitchen. "Okay, I'm sorry. Maybe I was the one who needed company. Last night wasn't the best for me either. My little sister cried herself to sleep."

I rubbed the bridge of my nose. While I felt bad about Kinsley, that didn't give him the right to break into my room in the middle of the night—despite not actually needing the breaking-in part.

Tea. I needed tea. Preferably something caffeinated.

After rummaging through the cupboard for my favorite chai blend, I put the kettle on before finally facing Nolan. The rising sun spilled through the kitchen windows, turning him a translucent gold like a man-shaped glass of apple juice. Although I was furious about my rude awakening, there were more important matters to discuss.

I crossed my arms. "Why didn't you tell me you were the reason I survived the crash?"

He tilted his head. "Would that have made you feel better?"

"Of course not."

"Then that's exactly why I didn't tell you."

I tightened my robe. "I don't remember the accident clearly. When I try to recall it, I get flashes of being underwater, but I'm not even sure those things really happened."

Images flooded my uncaffeinated brain. Darkness, a

glimmer of scales, arms wrapping around me, surging toward the surface, away from Nolan. I wondered about his protective powers. Did he somehow call upon ocean creatures to help?

"Are you also the reason I got to shore?"

He shook his head. "No. The protective bubble I'd formed around you would have dissolved the moment the car hit the water. The moment I died."

"Why didn't you save yourself too?" My tone sounded harsh, but I only felt angry that I was here and he wasn't.

"We were in a steel trap hurtling over the edge of a cliff into waters far below. My powers were limited. I had just enough to save one of us and a split second to do it."

And his instinct had been to save me. I nodded, not sure what else to say. To give myself something to do, I scooped tea into the infuser and poured the boiling water over it.

A few moments of silence passed before Nolan said, "I'm sorry for how my mom acted toward you last night, for what she said. But she didn't mean it. She was drunk and grieving."

That was probably true, but I'd always hated how he blew off the way his parents treated me. While he was only trying to keep the peace, did he know how much it hurt me? I guessed it didn't matter. It wasn't as if he could stand up for me now.

"She wasn't wrong, though." I snapped. "You died because of me."

Cold seeped into my shoulder as he tried to lay a hand on it. "I died *for* you. There's a big difference."

Gripping the edge of the sink, I fought back tears as I stared out the window. After the accident, the survivor's guilt had been bad enough, but at least I'd been able to say there'd been no control over it. Pure and terrible chance had taken my fiancé. It had been in the hands of something or someone much greater than us. Now that I knew the truth, I felt even more unworthy of the second chance he'd given me, unworthy of his sacrifice.

Too tired, too confused, I couldn't bring myself to look at

him. I needed space for once. He must have received the message, because he muttered something about checking on his family. When I turned around, I was alone, but I didn't call out or chase him. It would take time to digest this new information.

My tea had steeped too long. I rushed to dump out the leaves. After blowing on the dark liquid, I took a scalding sip. It tasted bitter, but it fit my mood at the moment, so I took another gulp.

Thuds from above told me Dad was awake. Not ready to tell him everything that had happened the night before, I slipped on a pair of shoes and stepped onto the back porch. The brisk morning air raised goose bumps on my arms. Inhaling deeply, I let it clear away the remaining sleep fog that lingered in my brain.

"You're up early." Helen's voice broke the silence.

I crossed the dewy grass to peer through the wrought iron fence and past the budding lilac bushes. The older woman was bent over in her flower-print coveralls, the tip of her white braid brushing the ground as she trimmed errant twigs.

I smiled. "I might say the same to you."

"After so many years of rising for school, it's habit," she said as she continued to work. "How is Alice?"

Of course she'd heard. If I didn't know gossip was a way of life in Hope, I'd have guessed it was Helen's witchy intuition. While I'd gone outside to be alone with my thoughts, what I really needed was to brainstorm my next step with someone I could be candid with.

I got right into it. "They think Alice poisoned Roman. Not to mention killed Caitlin and set the fire."

"What?" Helen straightened, wiping her creased brow. "That's ridiculous."

Part of me felt satisfaction that I'd surprised her with the news. "And that's not all. Something… inexplicable happened during the party."

"Nothing is inexplicable. Why don't you bring that chai over here and we can chat?"

I stared down at my mug. How had she smelled it from over there? Must have been a garden witch thing. Herbs were kind of her specialty.

Once I'd followed the fence around, I slipped through her front gate and crossed her yard. I passed beneath a pergola already sprouting clematis leaves and wandered into a practical maze of fruit trees, herbs, and vegetables. While everyone else's garden was still blinking its sleepy eyes after winter, hers was blooming. My dad probably viewed it as cheating. He prided himself on having a green thumb, but this was, well… magical.

As I crossed Helen's too-green lawn, she glanced up but continued her tending. "So?" she prodded. "Tell me about this inexplicable thing that happened."

I was still struggling to make sense of it. "Well, the guests were… angry."

She snorted. "I don't blame them. I'm sure last night was quite the display of wealth. For years, people have suspected the mayor of siphoning money from the town treasury. No one has proved it, but to see them showing off last night would have annoyed the taxpayers."

Her words reminded me of a few scathing comments I'd overheard on my eavesdropping mission. "Why does Quinton Abernathy keep getting reelected then?"

"Don't look at me. I didn't vote for him." She brushed the subject away. "So, was that all? Angry guests?"

I set aside the mental detour. One mystery at a time. "No. I mean, people were furious. Yelling, swearing, fighting. There were punches thrown. At an engagement party, for goodness' sake."

"That is strange." She dropped the leafy clippings into her woven basket, giving me her full attention. "What upset everyone so much?"

I turned my palms up helplessly. "Nothing that I noticed.

One moment, I was talking to someone, and the next, they stormed off to look for a fight. It was like a switch had been flicked."

Growing quiet, Helen rubbed her cheek, leaving dirt smudges behind. When she opened her mouth to say something, the loud clang of her front gate whacking the fence cut her off. We moved to investigate, but a moment later, my father stomped around the side of her home, housecoat flapping open to reveal his T-shirt and pajama pants.

"Dad? Is everything okay?"

He shoved branches aside with his cast while he balanced a plate of breakfast in the other hand, like he'd been in too much of a hurry to even put it down. "Violet, there you are. I knew you'd be with this… this witch. What nonsense is she filling your head with now?"

I winced at the word "witch" and peered around. The properties in Hope might have been large, with the houses spaced out and room to breathe, but he was yelling. If anyone had overheard him, hopefully, they'd assume he was merely name-calling.

Helen shook her sheers at him. "You listen to me, Stanley—"

He ignored her and pointed an icing-covered fork at me. "After everything I did to protect you, your continued relationship with this woman feels like a betrayal."

I jerked back. "I don't understand what the problem is. We're just talking."

While he hadn't warmed to the idea of me being a witch, he'd at least seemed resolved. So why the sudden outburst? It wasn't like we were dancing naked beneath a full moon, slaughtering virgins or anything.

"Didn't I provide you with a good life? I did the best I could on my own."

"Of course you did. I know that." Hesitantly, I reached out to him. "Where's this coming from?"

Dad flicked my hand away. "If you're not happy with me, then why don't you move out and live with her?" He waved his fork at Helen dismissively.

I exchanged a baffled look with her. "What's happening? The way he's acting is like…"

That was when I finally noticed his "breakfast." Two half-smudged pink sugar flowers lay on top of an ivory base. The extra cake I'd put in the fridge the day before.

I lurched forward and snatched it away from him. What were the chances that all the party guests had erupted with unprovoked rage, and now, Dad too? Jason's theory rushed back to me. Had I accidentally poisoned my father?

"How much cake did you eat?"

He crossed his arms. "I didn't see your name on it."

"Why don't you sit for a minute?" I said in a voice I'd use to soothe a wolf with its hackles raised. "I need to talk to Helen. Then, I'll go back with you to the house, and everything will be all right."

He grumbled and muttered under his breath but backed off to pace on Helen's tulips. She tensed as if ready to throttle him, but I held the plate in front of her.

"They think this cake poisoned Roman. People were acting exactly like this at the party." I kept my voice low to not further enrage my father. "Alice made too much, so she brought some over for us. After everything that happened, I forgot it was in the fridge. Should I call an ambulance or something?"

Forgetting about her tulips, she inspected the cake. "A poison that makes people angry?" She pursed her lips before swiping her finger through the dessert and sticking it in her mouth.

I gaped at her. "What are you doing? I just said this thing might be poisoned."

She licked a bit of icing off her lips. "Buttercream. Delicious but definitely not poison. It's a very chaotic magic."

"Magic?!" Dad roared. Moving onto the daylilies, he began a tirade about witches.

I ignored him. "Who magicked it or spelled it or whatever?"

Helen heaved a weary sigh. "The person who baked it, of course. If you weren't avoiding your studies, you'd understand magic better."

My mouth popped open. "Alice is magical like me?"

Where to start? It was shocking enough that my best friend was a witch. But one who wanted to poison half the town?

"I don't believe she did it on purpose," Helen said as though reading my thoughts. "I doubt she even knows she's a kitchen witch."

"A kitchen witch? What's that?"

"Her powers seem to manifest in her baking. With all the stress in her life right now, her magic is unstable and would have negatively affected any guest who ate her cake last night."

"And now, my dad." I tugged on one of my red curls as I watched him. "Is he going to be okay?"

She frowned at her crushed tulips. "The magic will wear off in time. Until then, he'll be more annoying than usual. We just need to keep him from doing anything foolish."

Now that I recounted the people I'd served cake to, it made sense why a sweet man like Milton Curry had joined the mob. Meanwhile, Jason and the sheriff, who'd passed on a slice, had remained levelheaded.

My resentment toward Christine Abernathy's outburst subsided. There was no doubt she'd meant every word, but she wouldn't have said it to my face if she'd been in control of her emotions. If every one of my barbed thoughts tumbled out of my mouth, I'd have more than a few apologies to make.

I was glad I hadn't eaten the dessert. If only Roman could have said the same. Then again, he hadn't become irate like everyone else. He'd died.

An idea struck me, one I hated to voice, but what choice

did I have? "Helen, if Alice can bake anger into a cake, could she also infuse it with the desire to kill someone specific?"

She considered me as if I wasn't completely hopeless. "Since we don't understand her powers yet, it's possible. That might be why Roman was the only person who died."

Even though I'd been the one to bring it up, I dismissed the idea. "Alice wouldn't want to kill someone."

"It's human nature to have angry and even violent thoughts from time to time without intending to follow through with them. But from the taste of this cake, Alice has the power to do it and doesn't even know it." Her brow knitted. "I'm afraid your friend's magic is out of control. She needs help. Go find her and bring her here."

"Oh, Alice." Had my bestie inadvertently killed someone?

CHAPTER SEVENTEEN

I raced to my room, where I changed into a sweater and a pair of jeans, not bothering to kick Zelda out first. She kneaded my quilt, grumbling about the early hour. However, when I left for Alice's place, she tagged along, perhaps for moral support. More likely, though, she was just hoping for drama. Unfortunately, when we arrived, that was exactly what we found—the sheriff's vehicle sat in the driveway.

A hiccup of panic seized my chest. Was Alice being arrested?

When I found her sitting on the front lawn, I relaxed. Then I noticed she was in her housecoat, staring at the slippers on her feet. So things weren't great, but at least she wasn't in handcuffs.

Someone sat next to her, half hidden behind the large oak tree. As I rounded the trunk and their head turned my way, I inhaled sharply. Max.

A flurry of emotions stirred inside me, more conflicted than usual after our confrontation at the party. When he got to his feet, I wondered if it was to pick up where he'd left off. However, his guilty expression and the way he worried his bottom lip told me the cake had worn off, and he was feeling the aftereffects of remorse.

Ignoring him, I sank to my knees in front of Alice. "Are you okay? What's going on?"

She lifted her red-rimmed gaze to mine. Her chin quivered before she covered her mouth, unwilling or unable to say the words. I wrapped an arm around her, and she rested her head on my shoulder.

Max knelt to pet Zelda, who was shamelessly wailing for his attention. "The sheriff has a warrant. I assume they're searching her house for whatever killed Roman."

"Well, they're wasting their time," I said, more for Alice's benefit.

"Trust me, I told them that. They informed me I should back off unless I wanted to be arrested." He leaned against the tree trunk and crossed his thick arms, glaring at the house.

I assumed the look was meant for Jason. I could only imagine how their conversation had gone down. The deputy would have jumped at the chance to lord his authority over Max.

Alice sniffled. "I wish I knew what they were doing in there."

Having gone through a similar experience when they'd searched the jewelry store, I understood what she meant. Someone ransacking a place close to your heart, rummaging through your precious things without care, was a special kind of psychological torture.

Zelda snorted. *Maybe you guys can't get inside the place, but what are they going to say to a cat?*

Of course, this would have sounded like normal cat meows to the other two, since they weren't in the witch club. Well, Alice was about to be. She just hadn't been initiated yet.

With one last aggressive rub against Max, Zelda twirled toward the door, head raised high. I opened my mouth to call after her but shut it again. She was the closest thing we had to a fly on the wall and had proved her cat burglary skills breaking into Roman's. Also, I needed to limit how often I conversed with animals in public.

Alice had gone quiet again, so I turned to Max. "Why are you here so early?"

"I came by to put some finishing touches on the kitchen." He thrust his chin toward the pickup truck parked along the street. A decal pasted to the side said One With Nature Carpentry. "When I arrived, they were kicking Alice out of the house."

Arm still around my friend, I gave her a squeeze. "Why didn't you call me?"

She gave a pathetic shrug of one shoulder. "I didn't want to bother you. You had a rough night too. And if not for me, you wouldn't have been at that party."

I winced, knowing the opposite was true. The Abernathys had only hired her because of me, because I'd wanted to spy on Nolan's family. "My night wasn't as rough as yours. I want to be here for you."

A jingle came from her housecoat pocket. She pulled out her phone and checked the screen. "I should take this."

She got up and walked away before answering. The longer she spoke with the person on the other end, the deeper the line between her brows became. I strained to listen in, but Max started speaking.

"Violet," he began. "I'm sorry for how I acted last night, for unloading on you. I'm not sure why…" The tanned skin next to his eyes tightened as though he were doing a complicated math problem. He shook his head. "It doesn't matter. I did it, and I'm sorry."

"You don't need to apologize. Really." After all, I'd already known about his lingering resentment, and it was the cake's fault he'd acted on it.

Everyone's inflamed emotions seemed to revolve around the thing eating away at them the most, like Christine's loss of her son, Dad's feelings about my witch status, and even Max's animosity over how I'd left. The last one only emphasized that I'd hurt my old friend more than I'd ever realized.

He plucked a blade of grass and twirled it absently. "I have a lot of guilt surrounding Nolan's death. Last night, I tried to put some of that onto you."

I glanced back at the house, but there was no sign of Zelda. And since Nolan wasn't around for once, it might be the only time we'd get to talk openly.

"Guilt over what?" I asked, afraid the answer was me.

His lips twitched in amusement. "I don't regret telling you how I felt, if that's what you're thinking. In fact, I should have told you sooner and not laid it on you right before the wedding. I am sorry about that."

I didn't miss the word "felt," as in the past tense. But it had been five years, a long time for feelings to change. So why was it suddenly so hard to breathe?

Max stared at his hands. "The real guilt was about Nolan. We were fighting a lot leading up to the wedding."

"You were?" That week had been a blur of heightened emotions and last-minute to-dos. Now that I thought back, though, I had noticed some tension between them.

He bobbed his head. "Things were pretty strained, and we both said some stuff. Stuff we can never take back."

That wasn't entirely true, but I couldn't tell him that. "For the record, I know I hurt you when I left, and I'm sorry I wasn't here."

The apology felt incomplete. However, if I said much more, the whole truth might spill out along with it, about Nolan being a ghost, his powers, mine, so I bit my tongue.

Max sighed. "You did what you had to do."

I gave him a grateful smile for his understanding. However, considering his outburst the night before, it was obvious some bitterness remained. I didn't know if we'd ever resolve things between us, but at least this was a start.

Alice plopped onto the grass next to me, her shaking hands clutching the phone. "That was a lawyer. Mayor Abernathy wants to sue me for the cost of the party and emotional damages."

Max stiffened. "What?"

I got up to pace. "How ridiculous. That's assuming you poisoned the cake, which you didn't. And since they have no proof, they have no case."

A whisper of grass announced Zelda's return from the house. *I wouldn't be so sure about that,* she sang.

The others paid her no mind, but I widened my eyes at her, fighting the urge to scream "Spit it out already."

She flicked her tail as if brushing off my impatience. *They just discovered a bottle of something in her kitchen. They're fairly certain it's the poison that killed Roman.*

My mouth fell open. I looked up at the house in time to watch the sheriff carry out a box of what I assumed was evidence. Jason shut the door behind him and secured yellow police tape in front of the steps. When he met my gaze across the yard, his mouth pulled down at the corners, and he turned away.

"They found the poison," I said without thinking.

Max narrowed his eyes at me. "How can you possibly know that?"

Yes. Zelda snickered. *Please, tell us how?*

"I'm just good at reading body language," I said.

"P-Poison?" Alice scrambled to her feet, body rigid like she was preparing to run. "They're going to arrest me for murder."

Max stood slowly, hands raised the way one might approach a skittish deer. "They won't arrest you. At least not yet. They'll have to test the contents of the vial and match it to whatever was in Roman's system. There's still time."

"Now? Later? What's the difference?" Tears filled her eyes. "I'm going to jail."

I gripped her by the arms. "No, you're not, because you

didn't do it. Somebody planted that vial in your house. We just need to figure out who's setting you up."

The presence of the poison was a good thing—sort of. Sure, Alice had temporarily cursed every guest at the party with her negative energy, but someone had gone to the trouble to frame her, which meant Roman had actually been poisoned. Alice hadn't killed him with her magic. There was still a bad guy out there, and I was going to find them.

She pursed her lips. "But who in that room would have wanted to kill Roman?"

A humorless laugh slipped out. "You'd be surprised. I've already been looking into a few people."

She blinked at me. "You've been investigating the murder?"

"Of course."

She launched herself at me and embraced me tightly. "I don't want you to get caught in the middle of this. If there's really a murderer out there and they want to pin it on me, they won't be happy about you trying to expose them."

"You're always taking care of everyone else," I told her. "It's time you let someone do the same for you."

Max stepped forward. "I'll help in any way I can. Just tell me what you need me to do."

"Thanks, guys." Alice wrung her hands like she didn't know what to do with them. "I feel so useless right now. The sheriff said my house is off limits, and I need something to keep my mind busy. Can I come over and bake for you and your dad, Vi?"

Leave it to Alice to turn to baking when things got tough. However, with her emotions in turmoil, it was the last thing she should be doing. Which brought me to the reason I'd come to visit her.

"Before you do any baking, there's someone you should talk to."

CHAPTER EIGHTEEN

After the sheriff so generously let Alice change into some clothing from inside her home, she, Zelda, and I headed back up Elbow Hill. However, when we bypassed my house and approached Helen's front door, Alice tugged me back.

"Wait. Why are we going to Mrs. Freeman's? I mean, she's a smart lady, but how can she help?"

She spoke in a hushed tone as though she didn't want to discuss her predicament with anyone else. Or maybe just our old elementary school principal. I didn't blame her. Despite being retired, Helen had never lost the ability to make our inner demons squirm.

"Trust me." I knocked on the door. "She knows more than you realize."

A moment later, Helen yanked open the door and ushered us inside. "Welcome, welcome. Come on in."

As we passed the sitting room, which was more of a greenhouse with all the plant life scattered around it, I spotted my dad sprawled on the floral couch. A puddle of drool had formed on the throw pillow beneath his head.

I pointed. "What happened to him?"

Helen waved a dismissive hand. "I gave him tea to help

him sleep off the effects of the cake. It was either that or one of us was going to wind up dead." She quirked one eyebrow, daring me to argue. "And I'm tougher than I look."

I didn't doubt it, so I kept my mouth shut. Since my dad was breathing easily and was no longer destroying her property, I supposed it was for the best.

She turned to Alice. "I hear you've been having a rough time."

Alice ducked her head, high cheekbones reddening like two apples. "Yes, Mrs. Freeman."

"It's gotten worse," I said. "They found the poison in her house this morning."

Helen's eyebrows rose to the tight beehive she'd arranged her hair into since I'd been there. "That's excellent news. It means she didn't kill him."

Alice's head snapped up. "Wait. I'm confused. Doesn't that mean I appear even guiltier?"

I linked an arm through hers and led her to the round wooden table covered in a lace cloth. "There's actually more to it. Helen will explain it better than I can."

The older woman chuckled. "You ignore my advice about training for weeks then try to dump this in my lap? Oh, no. This has to come from you."

"Me?" I recoiled. "But I'm a newbie. I'm not qualified. You're the master here. Isn't this, like, your thing?"

"There's no formal orientation to this, and she's your friend. I'll be back with some tea." She disappeared into the kitchen, ending the debate.

Eyeing me, Alice took a seat at the table. "Vi? What's going on?"

I sank into the chair beside her, struggling to find the words. "Right. Well, Alice. The thing is… I'll just come out and say it." I took a deep breath and blurted, "You're a witch."

A few moments of silence passed before her bottom lip jutted out. "That's the harshest thing you've ever said to me."

"No. I mean, an actual hocus-pocus, broomsticks-and-pointy-hat witch. Except you don't have to wear the hat. You're a kitchen witch. That's why you're so good at baking."

I stopped to gauge how she was taking the news. A series of unreadable emotions flitted across her face until she narrowed her eyes.

"You're pulling my leg to distract me from everything, aren't you? Like after my dad left, when you swore you saw a mermaid. We spent hours by the shore searching for it."

Sidetracked, I stared back in surprise. "I'd completely forgotten about that."

We'd been only ten years old. Had I really been fibbing for my friend's benefit? Or had a fish jumped and my fanciful mind ran away with me?

"Look," Alice said, pulling me back from the past, "even if I believed there's such a thing as witches, being a good baker doesn't mean I am one."

I could see this was going to take more convincing than it had taken for me, especially since Alice's magic was less obvious than mine. "It's not simply about yummy cupcakes or cookies. You can bake emotions right into them."

Dishes tinkled as Helen swept out of the kitchen with a serving tray of tea and snacks. "And because you're usually so cheerful, your sweets make people happy. That's part of what keeps them coming back."

Alice sighed. "Yeah, right. Tell that to Roman."

Helen set the tray on the table. Maybe she sensed Alice was a tough case, because instead of leaving again, she took a seat. "Tell me. How were you feeling when you were baking the cake for the engagement party?"

My friend focused on her twisting hands. "Well, I had a lot going on. Everything was riding on the event, so I was stressed about doing a good job. I was also afraid of going to jail since the sheriff had just paid me another visit. And, I suppose, I felt a bit angry."

"A bit?" I asked.

She slumped against the back of her chair. "Okay, a lot angry. I was so mad at Roman for firing me. I was frustrated that the sheriff suspected I set the fire. And I was furious at myself for getting into that situation, for spending all that money, for making my website public. I mean, how did I think I was ready to start a business?"

Again, I wondered how much of that was due to my pushiness. But if she was at all angry with me, she was too nice to say it.

Helen poured tea into delicate floral cups for us. "I tasted some of that cake, and I believe that with your heightened emotions, you passed your anger and hostility on to the guests who ate it. That was why everyone acted the way they did."

Taking a long sip from her cup, Alice seemed to consider the theory. "I'm still having a hard time swallowing the witch thing."

I didn't blame her. I hadn't believed Nolan when he'd confessed to having powers until he'd showed me physical evidence. Even then, I'd tried to explain it away. At least Alice looked too exhausted to run like I had. But how could I prove it to her? Introducing her to a ghost wasn't an option, and showing her Helen's locked cupboard filled with potions and herbs wasn't undeniable proof.

As I searched the room, my attention landed on Zelda. She was sprawled in a sunbeam shining through the gap in the curtains, which happened to be on top of my dad's chest. She rose and fell with each one of his loud snores, but her sharp gaze was trained on our group.

"Zelda, can you please allow Alice to hear you? She's one of us now, so it's okay, right?"

She rolled her yellow eyes. *Welcome to the club.*

Alice leaped out of her chair and stood behind it like she was ready to use it to defend herself. "Did the cat just… talk?"

I'm not just a cat, she practically hissed. *I'm a familiar.*

"S-Sorry to offend you?" Alice said uncertainly.

The feline licked her paws, much with the same air as someone checking their nails. *I'll forgive you. This time.*

Alice hesitated before lowering herself back into the chair. "I talked to a cat. So either the stress of this week has finally broken me, or you're telling the truth, and I'm a witch," she said, as though speaking it out loud might help it sink in. "And the engagement party blew up thanks to me." She gasped and sat straighter. "Is Roman dead because of me?"

"No," I said quickly. "Zelda saw the sheriff find a bottle of poison in your house. That means someone actually murdered him and is framing you."

"My cake made people say and do things out of character, though. What if I made someone angry enough to kill Roman when they normally wouldn't?"

Helen stopped buttering her scone and set the knife down with a decisive *clink*. "You didn't hand them the poison. Since they brought it with them to the party, that means it was premeditated. They'd planned on killing him long before they'd eaten your cake, assuming they ate it at all."

Alice didn't appear mollified. She buried her face in her palms. "But poor Kinsley and her fiancé. I ruined that couple's special evening. Not to mention, I probably destroyed a few other relationships."

I had to admit, I'd overheard a lot of harsh words exchanged between friends and couples. And more than one guest would have woken with a black eye that morning.

It was Helen who found a comforting response. "You can't blame yourself. I knew your parents their whole lives until they moved away, and they didn't have a lick of power between them. It must have skipped a generation or two. So how were you to know? I've been buying your baking for years, and even I couldn't tell it was magic."

Alice peeked between her fingers and eyed the slumbering man in the living room. "Did I do that to your dad?"

Helen clicked her tongue. "No, I did."

When she didn't elaborate, Alice peered into her teacup. It reminded me of when I'd sat across from the older witch and learned about my heritage. I took a sip from my cup to show her everything was okay.

She set down the drink anyway. "I wanted to make people happy with my baking, and here I am hurting them. Are my powers evil?"

Helen reached out and took Alice's hand in hers. "There are no good or bad powers. Only good or bad people. And you, Alice, are a good person. You simply need to practice, and there's no time like the present."

Gaping at the older witch, she yanked her hand away. "What? You want me to bake now? No. I don't want to hurt anyone else."

The motherly expression on Helen's face disappeared, and in the blink of an eye, she reverted to our elementary school principal. "Whether you like it or not, you have a gift. Last night, you discovered how dangerous it can be if you don't have control over it."

"I could just never bake again," Alice said.

The stern principal flicked her hand, shooing the idea away. "It's part of who you are. You might as well tell a fish to never swim again. Who knows what will happen if you suppress it for too long."

Alice turned her hopeless gaze to me. "Is your magic the same as mine?"

While I wanted to tell her all about Nolan and come clean about how I'd devised her ill-fated gig at Kinsley's party, I didn't want to get off track. Who knew how much time we had, so I kept it vague for now.

"My thing is ghosts. I'm connected to the spirit world, and because of my family's long history with jewelry and my passion for the art, it acts as my conduit. I'm pretty new to all this too. We'll learn together."

A hint of a grin peeked out. "Like we're back in school. We even have the same principal."

Helen stood. "Come now. I have a craving for your lemon squares."

With a deep breath, Alice followed her to the kitchen like she was marching to detention. Joining them, I hopped onto a stool at the island, where a variety of herbs grew in colorful pots of every size. As Helen emptied her cupboards onto the counter, Alice mixed ingredients as if on autopilot.

She seemed relieved to do something that took her focus off the mind-blowing news she'd received. Since I was no help in the kitchen, my thoughts returned to the night before, and I mused out loud.

"We have to assume the bakery fire and Roman's poisoning are connected, unless he was very unlucky. And since no one could guess what piece of cake you'd serve him ahead of time, the killer would have poisoned it immediately before he ate it."

Alice's mouth pulled to the side. "There were so many people around. It could have been anyone."

"Some more likely than others." I started at the top of my list. "What about Ingrid? She wants the baking contract with the new resort. What better way to get it than to burn down the rival bakery? When that wasn't enough, she took out Roman and framed you. Two fish, one hook. She was the first to know about your new business, after all, so maybe she's been keeping tabs on you."

From the other side of the island, Helen scoffed. "Ingrid? She's all bark and no bite—loud and incessant as a chihuahua."

"Well, what if jealousy was the motive? Did you know Roman was dating two women at the same time?"

She brushed that one off too. "Of course. Everyone knows that."

"Including them," I pointed out. "But I have to admit, I can't see it being either of them. I was standing right there when they watched Roman die. It would be hard to fake that kind of shock and grief."

While I wanted to dismiss them as suspects, the harsh words they'd exchanged once under the cake's spell made it clear not everything had been sunshine and roses. However, Pepper had wanted to break up, not kill the guy. Then again, that was what she'd want people to believe if she'd packed a bottle of poison in her clutch.

"What about Milton Curry?" I tried again. "Supposedly, there was bad blood between him and Roman. Something about a long-lost love. Do you know who that was?" I asked Helen, the older Hope resident.

A smirk played at her lips. She loved secrets and gossip as much as the next local. "It was a woman named Grace Merri-weather."

I blinked. "Roman's first partner in the bakery?"

Her expression grew sad, resembling Dad's when he'd recalled the woman's tale. "Milton was head over heels for Grace, but she was young, and she only had eyes for Roman. Desperate to get his attention, she came to me for a love potion."

Alice dropped a measuring cup, and the flour in it puffed into the air. "An actual love potion?"

I gawked at Helen, shocked for a different reason. "She knew you're a witch?"

"She didn't know—not really—but people talk. Some folks around here are more open-minded than you might think."

Wiping up the flour, Alice eyed her. "So did you give her a love potion? Is that even a thing?"

"Certainly, but they only work for a short time, and it's not a guarantee. The person who drinks it simply becomes open to the possibility of love. It nurtures feelings already present. But if the feelings were never strong enough in the first place, they fade. And the only person Roman ever loved was himself."

I nodded. "Grace was supposed to be a partner in the

bakery, but Roman's underhanded tactics left her with nothing. That brings me back to Milton Curry. Could he have loved Grace so much that he'd want to avenge her?"

Alice threw me a skeptical look over her mixing bowl. "Why would he do something like that now, after so many years?"

"Maybe losing his mother was one loss too many. Grief does strange things to people." I understood that all too well.

"I guess your next step is clear," Helen said. "Milton is the only person left from that love triangle who can answer your questions now."

She was right, but getting the reserved man to open up and gossip wouldn't be easy. Then, an idea struck me. I already had the perfect excuse to talk to him: his family jewelry.

I jumped off the stool and rushed into the living room to wake Dad from his tea-induced nap. There was work to do.

CHAPTER NINETEEN

Standing in front of Milton Curry's house with his jewelry in my leather bag, I fought the desire to bang on the cheerful yellow door as though the place were on fire. It certainly felt like an emergency.

Since it had taken Dad the rest of Sunday to complete the appraisal, my investigation had been delayed until the next day. Time was slipping away. I was terrified the lab report on the poison would come back at any moment, leading to Alice's arrest.

Reining in my impatience, I knocked politely. A moment later, the door opened, and Milton flashed me a friendly smile.

"Violet. Come on in." He gestured for me to enter. "I could have come to the shop and saved you from making a house call."

"Don't worry. It's all part of the service." Not exactly true, but it wasn't like I'd traveled a great distance, and I didn't want there to be any chance he might not show.

When Milton led me into the sitting room, I wasn't surprised to find his mother seated on the chintz sofa, which was adorned with cross-stitched pillows and a crocheted blanket. Something told me Milton hadn't changed a thing since he'd inherited it.

Not wanting to snuggle up next to her, I asked, "Is there a table we can sit at?"

Milton showed me to a dining room with an antique oval table. The extension leaf was still in even though he lived alone. A partially eaten TV dinner for one sat at the head of it.

He hurried to gather it. "Sorry about that. I haven't cleaned up from lunch. Can I get you anything to drink while I'm in the kitchen?"

"No, thank you."

As he carried the leftovers away, I took out a velvet cloth from my bag and spread it across the wood tabletop. One by one, I laid out the jewelry pieces he'd brought into the shop a week earlier.

Mrs. Curry huffed as she watched. "Figures. My son finally gets a woman to come by the house, and it's to sell my jewelry and cut out my heart."

Gee, this is going to be fun.

Although I'd quoted Milton two weeks for the appraisal, the opportunity to question him sooner had been too perfect to pass up. After I'd roused my dad at Helen's, he was sheepish and apologetic for what he'd said while under the cake's influence. As if trying to make it up to me, he practically ran to the store to get the appraisal done.

The incident still weighed on me, though. It was possible a dark part of him believed the thoughts he'd expressed, but his love for me usually kept them at bay. I'd reassured him the outburst hadn't been his fault, but he'd been moping ever since. I knew it would take time to repair things between us.

When Milton returned, he stood back, admiring the collection as if he'd never seen the jewels before. "Wow. I don't remember them being this sparkly."

"I gave them a cleaning. Pieces like these deserve to shine."

I pulled out the summary I'd put together based on Dad's

notes. The paperwork had our business header on it, far more professional than his scribbled notes on lined paper. I reviewed the details and value of each piece with Milton, noting the characteristics of the gems and metals.

His mother observed over our shoulders, adding her two cents. "My grandmother got that ruby necklace from a gentleman caller. She didn't marry him, but he showered her with treasures for a while. Gran was a looker in her younger years." She pointed at another piece. "That was the ring my great-grandfather proposed with. The women in our family have passed it down ever since."

It was history that she should have documented before her death, because I couldn't relay it all now. However, in addition to my dad's notes, I pretended to "guess" at other aspects of their history as much as I could without raising suspicion.

Milton hung on my every word. Once I'd finished, he thanked me profusely. I had a feeling it wasn't because I'd told him how much money he'd make by selling the collection but because I'd given him one more connection to his dearly not-so-departed mother.

"I'm just so surprised," he said. "The only jewelry she wore was her wedding ring. I didn't even know she had these until she passed. We had no money when I was growing up, and Dad died when I was young, so I don't think any were gifts from him."

His focus drifted to an old wedding photo on the wall, and I turned in my seat to study it. The woman in white was a fresh-faced representation of the ghost standing next to me. However, it was the groom who made my mouth fall open.

While he wore a suit instead of coveralls, and his torso was fully intact beneath his cummerbund, I recognized him from the hospital waiting room right away. "Is that your father?"

"Yes," Milton said. "He died in the cannery accident when I was a baby."

"That's so sad." And what was even sadder was that his

father's ghost had been stuck in the ER ever since, waiting for his turn to see a doctor. Or, more importantly, his maker.

The knowledge sat heavily on my chest. It was an awful secret, one that would only bring Milton pain. Not that I could say anything. His mother, on the other hand, might actually be able to do something about it. It brought to mind Nolan's suggestion that I help troubled spirits move on, the suggestion I'd immediately disregarded.

Putting it aside for later, I pressed on with the official work and placed each piece of jewelry in a velvet bag for safekeeping. "Since Charming Treasures has been in the business so long, we've developed a lot of connections. We can help you find buyers or put the items on consignment in our store. There are a few other shops in the area that will do the same, so check their rates and compare your options."

Mrs. Curry flung her hands up so quickly they blurred before reforming on her hips. "Here we go. You're nothing but a bamboozler. All you're worried about is money, you greedy thief."

I suppressed an eye roll and held up a pearl bracelet for Milton to consider. "But are you sure you don't want to keep them? I've seen a lot of jewelry in my life, and these are lovely heirloom pieces. I'm certain your mother left them to you in the hopes you'd pass them on."

This time, I risked a glance her way. Her focus was on her son, eyes filled with yearning as she waited for his answer.

He rubbed the back of his neck. "Like I said, I'm a bachelor. Always have been and probably always will be."

"Come on," I pressed. "A charmer like you must have had a special lady in your life at some point."

A slow grin spread across his face. "There was one. Her name was Grace."

Mrs. Curry made a disgusted, throaty sound. "Graceless, more like it. To think, she passed over my son for that slimeball, Roman."

"That's a beautiful name," I said.

"She was a beautiful person, inside and out." His attention shifted to the fireplace, where several photos cluttered the mantel. Grace's must have been up there. "Unfortunately, things didn't work out between us."

"Was it because of Roman?" I asked, trying to keep straight what he'd told me and what I wasn't supposed to have heard from his mother.

"Yes and no. She wasn't really mine to begin with. I regret not making a move, but my mother didn't approve of her."

The ghost sniffed indignantly. "I don't know. Looking back now, she'd have been all right. At least it would have meant I'd have a grandbaby, Curry blood or not."

I'd been so used to tuning her out that it took a moment for her words to sink in. And sink in they did. A baby? But not Milton's? So did that mean…?

I willed myself to act natural. "It seems you cared a lot for her. Why didn't you two work things out once Roman turned out to be, well, Roman?"

Milton chuckled, obviously appreciating the sentiment. If anyone could, it was him. "I think the whole experience broke her heart. She wouldn't date anyone after that. Roman was… Well, I don't want to speak ill of the dead. What's done is done."

His tone held a note of finality. I'd gotten as much as I was going to get out of him. However, it was clear his mother knew something, and she wasn't as tight-lipped.

I coughed and cleared my throat. "I think I've changed my mind about a drink if it's not too much trouble."

"Of course," he said. "What can I get you?"

I was about to say water, but I needed more time alone with his mother than that. "A cup of tea would be great. Whatever you have is fine. Thank you."

As he hurried to the kitchen, I clutched the pearl bracelet

still in my hand and rounded on Mrs. Curry, who was watching me like I'd steal something. As my gaze met hers, she flinched.

"Y-You can see me?"

"Yes, I'm just good at pretending I can't. Listen, we don't have long." There were so many questions I wanted to ask her, but since Alice might be arrested at any moment, I had to start with the most practical. "What you said before, about Grace. Did Roman get her pregnant?"

She glared at me. "What's it to you?"

Figured. She couldn't stop chatting until the moment you needed her to talk. "I have information for you, something that'll change your life. Or, rather, your afterlife. Please, tell me what I need to know, and I can help you."

It made my skin crawl to use her poor husband's ghost as a bargaining chip. One way or another, I'd tell her. For now, though, I'd let her believe it came at a cost; I didn't want to risk her refusing to spill the info.

Her lips pursed as she considered me. Finally, she clicked her tongue. "I suppose there's no harm in revealing it, since they're both dead. Yes. That silly girl got herself knocked up. She wanted to keep it, but her family was as proud and traditional as they come. Snobs, if you ask me. They sent Grace to visit extended family to have the baby, and when she came back, she was without the child."

My mind whirled with new possibilities. "Did Roman know he had a kid?"

"I don't think so. Or else he did and never cared. My Milton knew, though. Still wanted to marry her, but like he said, she was too heartbroken. Not over that oaf Roman but over her baby."

Until now, I'd been operating under the assumption Grace had no heirs, but a secret baby changed things. If she'd left her estate to the child, that entitled them to Roman's too, so long as he hadn't changed his will in the short time before his poisoning. And if their heir knew of the inheritance coming to them, then it was a motive to kill.

"Do you know the name of the baby or the extended family Grace stayed with?" I asked. "Even the gender would be helpful."

Mrs. Curry sneered. "No. I tried to keep any talk of her out of this house. My only concern was encouraging my boy to move on from her."

I slumped with disappointment, but the clattering dishes told me not to dwell on it; there was still the matter of her husband. "He's not the only one who has to move on. So do you and your husband." I pointed to the wedding photo. "I've seen his ghost. He's been in the hospital emergency room since the accident. You need to go to him."

Her mouth parted, but no words came out. Then her face crumpled, and she looked ready to cry. The expression made the woman seem so much younger, childlike even. "No. No, I can't. Milton still needs me. I won't leave my baby."

In life or in death, a mother was always a mother, even to a fifty-something-year-old. "He's a grown man. You have to trust you raised him right and he'll be okay on his own. Your husband is all alone and suffering. You could be together again."

She blinked rapidly, and her chest heaved with panicked breaths she didn't need. Before she responded, Milton returned with a tray. She grew uncharacteristically quiet as he and I sipped our tea and spoke of the improving weather and upcoming local events.

When we finally set down our empty teacups, Mrs. Curry tried to grab my arm. Her icy fingers sent tingles through me.

"It can't end like this." Her voice wavered. "My jewels to be sold, my baby dying alone. And here I'll remain, watching him live out the rest of his days eating TV dinners for one. Please, do something."

Although I wasn't sure what else I could do without making

things weird, I gave it one last-ditch effort with Milton. "I don't mean to overstep, but I was talking to Pepper Moon the other day, and she had a lot of sweet things to say about you. I think she's got a crush."

Mrs. Curry watched her son hopefully. "There's plenty of fish in the sea, that's what I always say."

He frowned. "Wasn't she Roman's girlfriend? Or... one of them?"

"It wasn't serious. Besides, after dating a man like that—may he rest in peace—I think she needs a person like you in her life. I bet she could use someone to talk to right now."

"Yeah." He brushed his thumb over his lower lip. "Maybe you're right."

"But if not her, I hope you don't give up on finding some-one. I bet it would put a smile on your mother's face to see you happily settled."

The woman's ghost sniffled. "Thank you."

Despite not getting more information, an immense weight lifted from my chest. Perhaps having the power to talk to spirits had its moments.

Milton moved closer to the fireplace and picked up a picture of his mother from the mantel. I was about to excuse myself and leave him to his thoughts when a different photo caught my eye. I gasped.

"I-Is that Grace?" I tried to control the shock in my voice, as though I were asking out of polite interest.

Not noticing my distress, he shifted his focus to the beau-tiful subject. "Yes. That's her."

It was the younger version of the woman with the long salt-and-pepper braid. The one I'd seen after the fire and then again at the engagement party, once the cake had hit the fan.

Grace Merriweather was a ghost.

CHAPTER TWENTY

As I returned to Helen's place, I wasn't looking forward to the "I told you so" that awaited me. But I deserved it. If I'd been practicing my magic, I might have realized Grace was a ghost from the start, and her presence at both crime scenes would have been a clue. However, now that I thought back, I recalled actually speaking with her after the fire. Maybe my brush with death in the burning bakery had made my powers stronger. *Oh, joy*.

When I walked into my neighbor's home, the enticing aroma of freshly baked goods made my stomach rumble. Alice had spent the night at my house since hers was still off-limits. First thing that morning, she'd resumed her lessons with Helen, and judging by the smell, it seemed they'd been "studying" nonstop.

I poked my head into the kitchen to find them deep in discussion. Whatever they were talking about was drawing Alice's eyebrows together.

When she finally noticed me, she set down the cookie she was icing. "Hi, Vi. I was just telling Helen about the times I think I unintentionally used my powers. Like, you remember the summer before my dad left?"

I smiled sadly even as my mouth watered at the memory. "You baked something new almost every day. My dad never figured out why I wouldn't eat supper when I came home after playing with you."

She focused on creating perfect pink roses with her piping bag. "Mom and Dad were arguing all the time, but when I baked for them, it made them happy, and the fighting would stop." She worried her bottom lip between her teeth. "I guess I was spelling them into staying together, because when school started again, and I couldn't bake all the time, Dad left."

Helen added a few sprinkles to the cookie. "It's natural for a child to want their parents to stay together. You were intuitive with your magic, even back then. That's why you'll be a quick study. If only all my students were so willing to practice." She quirked an admonishing eyebrow at me, an expression I was way too familiar with.

To avoid her intense scrutiny, I inspected a tempting cinnamon roll drizzled with cream cheese icing. My stomach growled again, and I picked it up to have a closer look.

"Don't eat that!" Alice slapped it right out of my hand.

It flew across the room and smacked into the wall, leaving a trail of icing as it slid down the wallpaper. When it finally landed on the floor, we all watched it as though it might explode.

I wiped the icing off my fingers like they were contaminated. "Practice not going well then?"

"Sorry. I don't know what would happen if you ate that. These powers are so unpredictable." Alice took in the various plates and containers that crowded the countertops, each holding a different treat. "I think we'll have to throw all of this out."

What a waste, Zelda said between loud chewing noises. *Because, mmm… these things are delicious. I don't know what you're so concerned about.*

We all turned to where the nuclear cinnamon roll had been

sitting on the floor. It was gone, replaced with a satisfied cat licking cream cheese icing from her whiskers.

I gasped. "Zelda! What did you do?"

What does it look like? I had a snack.

Alice hugged herself. "Aren't you worried about the magic? We don't know what they do yet."

I know what they do. They fill my tummy, which is empty since none of you have fed me all day. Besides, no baby witch's spell is going to affect a powerful being like me.

Tense silence fell over the kitchen as we watched the animal clean herself. It was quite the elaborate procedure. When it was done, she sat primly, staring back at us.

"Well?" I prodded. "How do you feel?"

Furry, I imagine.

I rolled my eyes. "We can be sure it isn't an antisarcasm dessert."

Why are you all so worried? It was tasty. I almost don't want to go eat a bunch of grass and throw up like I usually do after a big meal. She froze, ears flattening against her head. *Did I just say that out loud?*

My lip curled. "Umm, that's gross."

No. What's gross is that I farted on your pillow this morning. Her eyes widened, and she held a paw over her mouth. *I don't know why I said that.*

Revolted, I made a silent vow to never let the furball into my room again. "Okay, too much information."

Zelda's tail flicked in agitation. *I can't help it. I can't stop saying stuff.* She hissed at Alice. *What did you do to me?*

My friend covered her face with her hands. "This is hopeless. I can't run a baking business if all my customers get random magical side effects."

Helen pursed her lips, studying the feline as she would a science experiment. "Maybe it's not so random. Do you recall when you made this batch? You were talking to me about the time you brought cookies to class and caused everyone to dance nonstop for the rest of the day."

"It was our Halloween party. I thought a party meant fun and dancing," Alice defended her nine-year-old self. Then her shoulders drooped. "After that, Mrs. Hartford went on stress leave until January."

Helen waved it off. "Don't worry about that. She was never cut out for teaching. What I mean is, while you were baking those cinnamon rolls, you were opening up to me. You were at ease, comfortable sharing. I believe that your unguarded mental state created a sort of..."

I gasped. "Truth serum, er... cinnamon roll. Which is why Zelda is spilling her guts. That's perfect." I spun to face Alice. "Whoever framed you had a plan all along, and they've covered their tracks well. They're not going to confess out of the blue. We can use this dessert to get the truth out of them."

Helen held up a finger. "Careful. As I told Alice, there are no good or bad powers, but witches are defined by what we do. I learned that when I meddled in Grace's love life. Something I still regret."

She was right. It felt morally icky. "But it's to clear Alice's name and get justice for Caitlin and Roman. Surely, the good outweighs the bad. I'll only use them on the murderer, who, by the way, I'm close to finding." Quickly, I gave them a rundown of what I'd learned at Milton's. "The killer has to be Grace's child because I saw her at both crime scenes. I just didn't know who she was at the time—or that she was a ghost." I muttered the last part.

"You would have if you'd been honing your skills," Helen said.

There was the "I told you so." Ignoring the completely accurate admonishment, I thought back to the photo in Roman's home, seared into my brain by the shocking way Zelda had put it there. Since he'd spent his entire life using and throwing women away, for that one to take up space in his bachelor pad meant she was important to him. While it could have been an old photo of his mother or another relative, there was a good chance it was a daughter.

I turned to Zelda. "Can you please show them the photo you saw in Roman's house?"

Okay, but it's going to cost you another can of tuna. Also, you'll have to clean up the grass puke, because I plan to do it on your porch.

Groaning at her disgusting honesty, I gestured for her to go ahead. A moment later, Alice yelped and groped the air like someone had shut off the lights.

"Have either of you seen that woman?" I asked.

Looking unbothered, Helen shrugged. "Not that I remember."

Alice rubbed her eyes as though trying to rid herself of the image. After a nervous glance at the feline, she focused on me again. "I have. Once. I went into Spread the Word late to do some prep work for the next day, and Roman was drinking in his office, looking at the photo. I assumed she was an old love of his, but it could be a daughter."

I'd hoped for more, but if neither of them recognized her, then it was unlikely she lived on the island. However, that didn't mean she'd never been there. She could have slipped in on a ferry, hidden among the early-bird tourists, and crashed the engagement party to kill Roman.

Zelda checked her claws casually. *There is one person who knows the answer to the whole love-child question. Grace herself. And in case you've forgotten, you can communicate with her.*

I shifted uncomfortably at the idea of collaborating with the dead. "I've only ever run into her when there was trouble. I wouldn't know where to start looking."

Then ask Nolan to track her down. He can cover more ground than you. Or is he yet another ghost you're avoiding?

Alice stared at me, mouth parted. "Nolan is a ghost?"

Loud banging on the door made all three of us jump. As though it were gunfire, Zelda zipped across the room in a blur and disappeared down the hallway to Helen's bedroom.

Normally, she'd love to eavesdrop, but with the spell in place, there was a chance she'd overshare with the visitor. That was the last thing any of us needed.

The banging came again, harder and more insistent this time. We all shared a look before Helen opened the door. It was Sheriff Reed and his deputy.

Mouth set into a grim line, Jason spun his wide-brimmed hat in his hands as if driving an out-of-control car. He studied the floral rug as the sheriff took out a pair of handcuffs and closed them around his cousin's wrists. Her body deflated like a bad soufflé.

"Alice Wright," Reed began, "you're under arrest for the murder of Roman Fedoro and Caitlin Sundry."

Rattling off her rights, he ushered my friend out of the house. I chased after them, only to stand in the middle of Helen's lawn, feeling utterly helpless as they loaded my BFF into the SUV and took her away. What was I to do?

Zelda brushed against my leg, probably out of feline instinct. It certainly wasn't to show emotional support, judging by the way she asked, *How's that one-woman investigation going?* Then, as if her point wasn't clear enough, she fixed me with a withering golden glare. *You're a fool.*

Thanks to the cinnamon roll, she had no choice but to tell the truth, so I couldn't argue with her. I had been a complete fool, whose BFF was going to jail because I'd refused to embrace my powers. Some friend I was.

CHAPTER TWENTY-ONE

By the time I'd raced down the hill and arrived at the sheriff's office, I was clutching my side and sucking in air. I rushed to the front desk, but no one was there. It was just after five. The admin assistant would have gone home for the day. I dinged the service bell on the desk three times and waited for as long as humanly possible—about ten seconds—before dinging it again.

Brisk footfalls thudded from somewhere deep inside the building. A door swung open, and Jason strode through. I breathed a sigh of relief it wasn't Reed since he wouldn't have given me the time of day. Or worse, he'd have arrested me for sticking my nose into his investigation again.

Jason stared at me in surprise. "Vi. What are you doing here?"

I gripped the sleeve of his shirt as if I could force him to hear me out. "You know Alice didn't do it."

"What I know and what I can prove are two different things. The lab reports came back. The poison in Roman's system matches the contents of the vial found in her kitchen."

"Have you considered that someone planted it there?" I asked. "When Roman died, there were at least half a dozen other people around him who might have wanted him dead. What about Ingrid or the two girlfriends he'd jilted that very night or Milton Curry?" I hated to throw everyone under the same bus at once, but I was desperate to give him even a moment's pause to see another possibility.

He didn't pause, however. "We found the poison in Alice's house. It doesn't get more clear-cut than that. No one had more motive or as much opportunity as she did. All the evidence points to her. We wouldn't be doing our jobs if we ignored that." His jaw clenched, and he dropped his gaze to the floor. "Look. If you have information, then say it. If you can do something, do it. But my hands are tied."

I wanted to beg or yell, but he seemed resolved. At least his puffy eyes and red nose proved he hadn't reached that resolution easily. And in any case, what was I supposed to tell him? There was a ghost out there who knew the killer?

When I said nothing, he lumbered into the back again, posture hunched. The anger that had ferried me down the hill leaked out whoopee-cushion style, and I left. I wasn't ready to admit defeat and go home, but I couldn't search for Grace until dark, and since the sun was staying up later and later, that wouldn't be for a while.

I crossed the street and wandered into Dolphin Park. The green space stretched between the downtown core and the ferry terminal, curving with the harbor's arched terrain like a dolphin jumping out of water. I walked until I found a bench where the seawall dipped briefly to form a sandy beach. Leaning against the backrest, I closed my eyes and massaged my temples.

"Come here often?" a man asked.

I jolted and nearly fell onto the ground before I recognized the voice. I squinted at the other side of the bench, where a barely visible Nolan relaxed in the dappled shade of a nearby tree. One arm slung across the back, suit jacket buttons undone, he looked like a model on location for a photo shoot.

"Nolan, what are you doing here?"

"Zelda filled me in on what's going on. She thought you might need someone to talk to."

He shifted his chin toward a black streak tearing across the open grass. The cat sprang into the air, doing acrobatics as she tried to catch a bird, and a large one at that. A hawk.

Had she really tracked Nolan down out of concern for me, and despite the occasional manipulation, she wasn't the worst? Or maybe she'd actually found him to tattle on me, and he was reframing the situation to keep the peace.

"But if you still need space," he added, "I can go."

I heaved a sigh. "Please, don't. I'm sorry I've been pushing you away."

He considered my expression before staring out at our seaside view for a painfully long moment. Finally, he threw me a bone. "It can't be easy being back, facing me again. And I know I've been pressuring you about my case."

"It's understandable," I said. "You've been stuck here for five years, eager to move on. Meanwhile, ever since I got back, I've been dragging my feet to come to terms with everything." I stared at my palms as though I might see them glow with magic. "But watching Alice jump into lessons made me realize how selfish I've been. You were right. I should be helping souls move on, not avoiding them. Avoiding you."

"In your defense, Alice gets to make delicious desserts, and you—"

"See dead people?" I laughed humorlessly. "Yeah, not the jackpot of magic skills. But it's more than that. I've been anxious to make up for things."

"Because you've been gone so long?"

"That's part of it," I said, uncertain how best to explain it. "Mostly, I'm afraid I've squandered the second chance you've given me. I feel as if I should be doing more to pay it forward, like how I've been working extra hours for Dad or supporting Alice and her business. And Max… Well, I don't know how to help him yet. I just feel like there's so much I need to do that I don't know where to begin. Solving the day-to-day problems has been easier than facing the paranormal stuff, so I keep putting it on the back burner and pretending I'm better off without it."

Nolan leaned closer and laid a hand on the bench next to where mine rested, the closest he could come without giving me a chill. "I saved you so you would live your life. Not so you'd live it for others. Stop worrying about this sense of cosmic payback and start living for you again. Well, after you've fixed things for Alice."

I raked my fingers through my curls. "That's been the problem all along. I thought I needed to fix everything for her. Her job, her business, her life. But I've only made things worse. And if I'd focused on practicing my magic, I might have found the killer much sooner."

"Ah, yes," he said. "Zelda told me about Grace Merri-weather too."

As though her ears were ringing, his familiar gave up on the hawk that was now mocking her from the top of a lamp-post. She padded over to us and curled up next to the bench to munch on grass. I recalled her earlier honesty and dreaded the cat sick I'd be cleaning up later.

I turned my attention to the waves frothing against the beach. "It never occurred to me Grace was a ghost. When I first ran into her, she reacted like she knew me, but she was probably just surprised I could see her. Then, after the fire, I thought Jason talked to her, but he'd been speaking only to me." I twisted to face Nolan. "I have to find her. Did you still want to be my Watson? I can't do this without you."

He puffed up his chest. "Of course you can't. That's why I already went searching for her."

I shook my head in amazement. "I really have been a stubborn fool to keep you out of the loop, haven't I?"

"Yes, but I knew you were stubborn when I proposed." He

winked before growing serious again. "Grace is at her old house. Unfortunately, I couldn't get much out of her. Not really a social ghost, I guess. That must be why I've never seen her around town."

My leg bounced from pent-up energy. I craved action. "Which makes me even more certain her son or daughter is involved. Why else would she have left her home to hang around both crime scenes?"

"I think you could get her to open up," he said. "Ghosts linger because of unfinished business. While she has no incentive to talk to me, you're able to do things for her, fulfill whatever task is keeping her from moving on. I'll come as your interpreter."

"It's an option, but it would be better if I could talk to her directly. That's the strangest part about our interaction the night of the fire. I heard her speak." Gnawing on my lip, I searched for an explanation. "I've been thinking about it, wondering if my powers are somehow getting stronger."

His cheeks quivered as he fought a grin. "You'd have to actually practice for that to happen."

"Then how do you explain it? To speak with a ghost, I normally have to touch…" I sat straighter. "Her jewelry."

I slapped my forehead. Why hadn't I realized it before?

"I found a broken charm in the alley. My hand was in my pocket, touching it, when she approached me. It had been hers. That's why I was able to communicate with her."

"You picked it up?" He looked incredulous. "Without knowing if it was evidence?"

I groaned. "Not the point."

"You're right. This means you can talk to her and clear everything up. If nothing else, she was possibly a witness to both crimes. Where is the charm now?"

My hope, which had been rising, came crashing down. "I handed it over to the sheriff."

I rubbed a palm over my face and considered the view.

That is, until I heard a strange noise by my feet and peered down in time to witness Zelda bring up a pile of grass and cinnamon roll. At least it wasn't on my porch.

As I observed her, a plan formed in my mind. "Thankfully, I know of a pretty good cat burglar."

Zelda gave me an indignant look—as though she had any dignity left after her disgusting display. *You want me to steal evidence from the sheriff's office?*

"Yes. It's the only way for me to speak to Grace directly."

It'll cost you more tuna.

I raised an eyebrow. "How about I let you off the hook for gassing my pillow?"

Fine. But I won't promise not to do it again.

Because I needed her help, I didn't argue with her. That was a fight for another day. Perhaps Helen had some antifamiliar potion I could spray around my room.

"All right. Let's get moving." I avoided the green puddle in front of me as I made for the street.

Nolan followed me, buttoning his jacket. "So? What do we do, Sherlock?"

I smiled. It felt good to have a partner in crime. "We'll head to Grace's and try to speak with her. But first, is someone currently living in her house? I want to know what I'm walking into."

"No one was home, but judging by the used coffee cup on the counter and food in the fridge, it looks like it. The furniture is dated, though, as if they're Grace's belongings."

I recalled what my dad had said about the property. He might have thought the place was empty because it had been quietly transferred to Grace's beneficiary. And since it was on the outskirts of town, word about someone living there likely hadn't spread yet. My money was on the blond woman in Roman's photograph.

"Do you know if it's a man or a woman?"

He threw me a sardonic look. "I didn't stick my head into

their underwear drawer to find out. I'm not that kind of ghost."

"Do those kinds of ghosts exist?" The idea sent shudders rippling through me. "Actually, never mind. I don't want to know."

When we reached the sidewalk again, Zelda branched off toward the sheriff's office. I called after her and told her to meet us at my place.

Nolan, who was already heading in the opposite direction, paused. "But Grace's house is this way."

"I know." I smirked. "It's poor etiquette to welcome a newcomer empty-handed. I'm thinking cinnamon rolls are in order."

CHAPTER TWENTY-TWO

Grace's home sat by the sea, miles from the nearest house. It was as though socially isolating herself hadn't been enough. She'd needed to physically remove herself from town as well. As I trudged down a driveway reclaimed by nature and listened to the birds cry over crashing waves, I sensed a different type of connection. After all the heartache she'd endured, I could see the appeal. However, now wasn't the best time for solitude— not when all I had for company was a ghost who could do nothing but watch if things went wrong.

Nolan scanned the quiet property as if he were my body- guard. "What's the plan?"

"It would be ideal if no one was home. I want to talk to Grace alone first."

I pressed a palm over my chest. The letter "A" charm hid beneath my T-shirt, dangling from a chain I'd borrowed from my jewelry box. I'd wanted a way to touch the conduit without it being visible to whoever lived in the house now. If they really were the arsonist, then they'd once worn the charm and would recognize it.

"What if someone answers the door?" he asked.

"Then I hope they're not gluten intolerant." I patted the

container of honesty-inducing cinnamon rolls that I'd grabbed from Helen's.

While I took her earlier warning seriously, I didn't see what choice I had but to use them. Just in case she disagreed with my assessment, though, I'd taken the treats when she was busy in her garden. She hadn't tossed the batch out, so I figured it wasn't against some witch law to use them in an emergency. And this was an emergency.

"I don't like this," Nolan said for the third time. "It's too isolated, and there's no cell reception. Can't you come back with someone? Even Zelda would be better than me."

"And tear her away from her posttuna nap? I prefer my face without claw marks, thank you. Besides, if I came with an army at my back, I wouldn't be invited in."

A screech tore through the sky. A hawk swooped above us, catching bugs that danced in the evening light. It dove and landed on a fence post, fixing me with a piercing gaze. Those unusual blue eyes reminded me of the hawk I'd spotted near the resort, like it was keeping tabs on me. But of course, it couldn't be the same bird. That would be too much of a coincidence.

There was no vehicle parked anywhere in sight, but since very few people in town owned one, that didn't mean someone wasn't home. Steeling myself, I marched up to the house and knocked. A moment later, the door squeaked open, and I sucked in a breath as the home's new occupant stared at me. Colette Roche.

Was I at the wrong house? This wasn't the woman from Roman's photograph. My attention shifted past her and into the home, where Grace fiddled with her braid. Now that the two of them stood side by side, the familial resemblance was obvious. They had to be mother and daughter.

Colette crossed her arms. "Good evening. May I help you?"

I gave her my cheeriest smile. "Consider me the Welcome

Wagon. Now that you've had time to settle in, I wanted to come for a visit and get to know you better."

Her frown deepened, so I offered up the container of goodies. Heaving a sigh, she waved me inside with a delicate hand.

"Come in. I will make some coffee."

At the mention of caffeine, I remembered it was late for a social call. However, I'd spent enough time in France to know her suppertime probably wasn't for a while yet. Before she changed her mind, I followed her inside.

The place was small and simple, with faded sofas, a worn rug, and an ancient TV that had likely belonged to Grace. It must have remained untouched since her death.

Nolan immediately joined the previous home owner, murmuring something too low for me to hear. As he spoke, her fidgeting hands stilled, and she watched me with interest.

Colette took the container from me. "How do you like your coffee?"

"Actually, do you have any tea?" I asked, hoping she'd make both and give me more time alone with Grace.

"Yes. I will be just a moment."

As she disappeared into the kitchen, which was blocked from view, I drew closer to the anxious ghost watching from the corner of the room. I took out my necklace and clutched the charm, not because I needed to but because it made me feel closer to her. Now that I knew who lived in this house, it became clear it wasn't a letter A. It was the Eiffel Tower worn down with age, the lines and details faded.

Grace's attention flitted to the kitchen and then back to me. "What are you doing here? Are you here to take away my baby?"

I cringed at her shrill tone, as though Colette might over-hear. "She's hurt people, hasn't she? Done things? The fire, Caitlin, Roman?"

Eyes brimming with tears, she tugged on her braid. "You

can't take her. I won't let you. Haven't we been separated long enough?"

Nolan laid a hand on her shoulder, a comforting gesture only he could manage. "You need to tell us what she's done. It's for her own good. What if she hurts someone else and gets into even more trouble? We can end it before things get worse for her."

Her misty gaze darted between the two of us. "She won't. She didn't do anything. Not my baby. I only wanted what was best for her. No. No. No." She whipped her head back and forth until her features blurred.

Dishes clinked as Colette prepared our drinks. Reluctantly, I spun away from the unhelpful ghost. It was up to Alice's baking now. I took a seat at the dining table set beneath an open window, started a voice recording on my phone, and placed it face down. I'd need evidence of Colette's admission and not just my word.

She returned a moment later, carrying a tray with two mugs and the container of cinnamon rolls. When she set a plate in front of me, I discovered a fatal flaw in my plan. With dread, I watched as she used a knife to separate two rolls from the rest. One for her and one for me.

Of course, she'd offer me a treat. It was good manners.

Can I fake a gluten allergy? No, of course not. She'd sold me enough baked goods to see through that lie, and refusing it would look fishy.

I played it safe by taking a sip of tea then remembered I was sitting across from a probable poisoner and set my mug aside. "Please, tell me what you think of the dessert. It's an old family recipe," I lied.

She finally took a bite, and her shapely eyebrows rose. "Good. For a novice."

Like much of what she said, I wasn't sure if I should feel insulted. However, it was possible the brutal honesty was due to the treat working its magic—literally. "Thank you. That means a lot coming from a woman of your talents."

She gestured to my plate. "Please, do not make me eat alone."

Nolan's hand shot out as if to snatch the dessert away. "Don't do it, Vi. This is a bad idea."

He was right, but if I refused, she might grow suspicious. I wasn't sure how the spell worked, but I needed her to remain relaxed enough to spill her secrets. And I supposed, if I wanted her to be vulnerable, I had to show my own vulnerability in return. So I picked up my cinnamon roll and took a tiny bite before washing it down with a chug of hopefully-not-poisoned tea. Maybe it would dilute some of the effects.

"So," I began. "What initially drew you to Hope City besides the resort? You didn't think it was an actual city, did you?" It wasn't exactly the Spanish Inquisition, but I wanted to test the magic slowly.

Colette shook her head. "My birth mother, Grace, used to live here. Thanks to her wretched family, she did not raise me, but she always kept in touch. She died several years ago from cancer." She swallowed hard before continuing. "If I had known how bad her condition was, I would have come to be with her. She did not deserve to die alone."

"I'm sorry to hear that. I didn't know her… in life." I felt compelled to add the last part, since I technically knew her as a ghost. Okay, so the magic worked. I had to choose my words carefully.

"I had planned to move here one day so we could open a bakery together. The way she talked about this place made it sound like heaven."

Something blocked the evening light slanting across the table. A rhythmic whooshing of air filled the silence, and I looked out the open window as my hawk friend landed on the planter fixed beneath it. The bird leaned closer, eavesdropping on our conversation.

Colette shooed it away as if it were not a magnificent bird but a rat with wings. "However, this place is a dump."

I flinched like she'd personally insulted me. "It's not for everyone," I said, sticking with a truthful reply that would satisfy the spell but not give me away. "Did your father live here too?"

She sneered. "I never knew who he was. Did not care to. My mother told me he was a terrible man. To protect me from him, she lied about my name. Even gave him a fake photo."

So that explained the picture in Roman's home. My instinct was to suspect she was lying about knowing him, but considering how hard I was battling Alice's magic, she had to be telling the truth. She was completely clueless Roman had been her father.

"Why did you want to work for Roman Fedoro?"

"Please." She snorted. "Like I would want to work for that talentless hack. I have more skill in my pinky finger than he had in his whole body."

"Then why apply at the bakery?" I pressed.

She went quiet, staring at the hawk, which had found a perch on the crumbling white picket fence. Was she fighting the spell? I worried she would clam up, but she eventually met my gaze.

"My mother and Roman were business partners. The second they started doing well and he had all her recipes, he cut her out. She tried to fight it in court, but then she received the diagnosis. What little money she had left she used on treatment. There was not enough." The muscles in her jaw worked as she clenched her teeth. "She died destitute and alone because of him."

"Is that why you killed him?" The question slipped out. I bit my lip, but it was too late. Had I blown it?

"But of course." Colette barely batted an eyelash. "At first, I only wanted to watch him suffer, to take away what he loved most, as he had done to me. I began by paying off the delivery driver to skip Spread the Word's supply shipment, thinking I would take him down slowly from within. However, Roman must have paid him even more for Ingrid's ingredients and to have the man claim hers did not come. So I tried to burn down his precious bakery."

I gaped at her. Did she even realize what she was saying? "And Caitlin? Did you strangle her?"

She huffed a breath through her nose. "That little thief was there to rob the place. She caught me in the act, so…" She shrugged. "Then your friend Alice arrived and tried to put out the fire, so I knocked her unconscious. She was in the wrong place at the wrong time. But for me, it was the right time, since they suspected her."

A sob escaped Grace. Nolan drew close to her and spoke in a hushed tone, but she only covered her face and cried harder. Perhaps she'd been holding onto hope or even denial until now, but she must have suspected. That's why she'd been there after every incident.

Colette gestured to me. "Then you came along and stopped the fire from destroying the building. You ruined my plan, so I had to continue working for that slob, slaving away in his truck."

"You didn't stop there, though, did you?" I asked.

"I knew it would never be enough. Even if I burned the bakery to the ground, he would simply rebuild. But my mother was gone. Forever. There was only one way to make him pay."

That was why the broken charm had felt so hostile, filled with anger and vengeance, yet so kind. Colette had been wearing it, and I'd sensed her anger toward Roman layered over the personality of the previous owner: Grace. However, when I'd touched her bracelet in the food truck, it presented a different Colette, one who'd come up with a new and calculated plan since the fire.

"So," I said. "You killed Roman and set up Alice."

As though we were still having a friendly visit, she nibbled the cinnamon roll. "Your baker friend was a convenient cover. She was already under suspicion for the bakery girl's death and the fire. Since I attended the party with Roman, it was easy enough to douse his cake with the poison I had been slipping him all week. I later planted the bottle in Alice's house." She sniffed. "People here are so trusting. They do not even lock their homes."

"Probably because we don't have a lot of murderers around here," I said, no longer hiding my true disgust with her. Both because I'd gotten the answers I'd come for and because the magic was in full effect now. There was no holding back anymore. "Just one problem. You've told me everything."

Oh, good. Way to point it out, Vi.

Nolan stepped closer. "Umm, I think it's time to go."

I agreed, especially since I'd just explained to her I was a liability.

Colette frowned. "Why did I tell you all of that?" Shoving her chair back with a scrape, she stared at the half-eaten dessert in horror. "What did you do? Have you poisoned me?"

Wouldn't that have been poetic? "No, I put you under a spell." I slapped a hand over my mouth. *What did I just say?*

Her eyes widened. "Who are you?"

My muffled response slipped from between my fingers. "A witch."

Stop talking. Stop talking. Stop talking.

She backed away. "You are strange. This whole town is strange. I wish I had never come here."

Unable to help myself, I laughed despite my growing dread. "Don't worry. We all feel the same way."

"But you are right." She grew calm again. "I suppose I will have to kill you now too."

And unfortunately, I knew for a fact she wasn't lying.

CHAPTER TWENTY-THREE

Colette's focus flicked to the serving tray, where the knife lay next to the cinnamon rolls. My heart smashed against my ribcage as I prepared for a fight. A second passed, then we both lunged at the same time.

She beat me to it.

"Run!" Nolan yelled.

He leaped in front of Colette as if to block her, and I dashed for the door. She blew right through him. Cutting me off, she raised her arm. Metal glinted as she slashed the knife downward.

Pain lanced across my upper arm and shot to my fingers. Screaming, I grabbed the wound. Panic surged through me, raw and electric. I couldn't think—I could only react.

When she came at me again, I kicked out. My boot landed on her hip, sending her flying back into the entertainment stand. A lamp on top of it teetered and fell, clipping her arm. It gave me enough time to put the threadbare sofa between us. However, now, she stood between me and the exit.

Grace wailed like a banshee, begging her daughter to stop. Nolan sank into a low stance, arms spread like he was about to take action but wasn't sure what to do or how to do it.

I scanned the small home. There was a back door, but it was secured with a deadbolt. It would take precious seconds to open it. Seconds that meant life or death. My phone sat on the table, where it was still recording, but it was no good unless I found cell service before I was stabbed to death.

Colette feinted as if to round the sofa, then she doubled back. I mirrored her movements and circled the room, always keeping furniture between us. Round and round we went.

Desperate, I threw anything within arm's reach: mantel photos, a vase of silk flowers, porcelain dog figurines. This infuriated her more. These weren't merely things. They were mementos of her late mother, all she had left of her.

As we danced around the room one more time, I spotted an urn, and an idea came to me. A terrible, truly awful idea but maybe my only chance. Still, the thought of threatening poor Grace's last physical tie to this world made me pause.

While my focus lingered on the urn, Colette vaulted over the back of the couch. She launched off the cushions in an arc, knife extended, straight for me.

Nolan darted forward. "Violet!"

"Sweetheart, no!" Grace hollered.

My stomach plunged, and my limbs locked in terror.

A high-pitched screech filled the house. For a moment, I thought the sound had come from me until a streak of brown and white shot through the open window and zipped past.

Wind gusts blasted my face. Wincing, I threw up my arms.

Colette screamed, and I dared a peek. My brain took a second to decipher what I was seeing. She writhed on the floor, caught in a flurry of feathers and hair.

The hawk, my hawk, was attacking her.

After a beat, I shook off my surprise and ran for the exit. Just as my hand gripped the door handle, the bird cried out.

Thud.

I risked a glance back. The magnificent bird flopped along

the floor in an awkward shuffle, wing held at an angle. It tried to take flight, bumping into the sofa then the table.

With a shriek of triumph, Colette grabbed a nearby laundry basket and dumped out the clothes in one swift motion. She slammed it down over the bird and drew her leg back to kick it.

"Stop!" I cried.

Without thinking, I moved away from the door, from freedom, and grabbed the urn. I held it above my head, and a fresh wave of spasms rippled down my arm. Gritting my teeth, I pushed through the pain.

"No!" Colette lurched toward me.

I tensed as though ready to smash her mother's remains onto the floor. A whimper escaped her, and she froze. I had her attention.

Sounds of the hawk struggling to free itself filled the silence. At least it was still alive, but I wasn't sure what my plan was. Delay Colette long enough for the bird to find its way out the window? Then what? All I knew was I had to derail her.

"Roman Fedoro was your father," I said.

Colette jerked back. "You lie." Her lip curled with a sneer. "He was always breathing down my neck, asking me out. That disgusting pig was not my father."

Grace's crying died, and she grew still. Covering her mouth with a hand, she looked between us. I'd just revealed her greatest and most shameful secret.

I couldn't help but note the contrast between her horror and Roman's behavior at the engagement party. He'd acted so happy, so boastful, so proud. But not the kind of proud that came from scoring a date with Colette. It had been different somehow. And when his spirit had spoken to her before moving on, his sadness seemed too profound for having met her only days before. Unless… he'd known who she was.

Things began to align in my mind. The new theory

explained why he'd been reviewing his will and why he'd invited her to the party instead of one of his girlfriends.

"When you came here, I think he recognized you," I said, working it out as I went. "You share your mother's looks, you love to bake like she did, and you're living in her house. Roman was a lot of things, but he wasn't stupid. He recognized his own daughter."

Colette's nostrils flared as though she smelled something rotten. "*Non. C'est impossible.*"

"Those weren't dates he was asking you out on. He just wanted to spend time with you and get to know you." My tired muscles shook, and I lowered the urn, cradling it in my good arm. "Roman's life was shallow and unfulfilling, and he pushed everyone away, including your mother. He must have had a lot of regrets, but I think not being a part of your life was his biggest one."

Her features turned stony. "You cannot know that."

"I've seen the fake photo of you he keeps in his home. I also learned he left everything to Grace in his will, but she's been gone for a long time, which meant he wanted it all to go to you. The one person he loved, in his own way."

As I spoke, understanding dawned on me. I'd been wrong about why Roman's ghost had crossed over. It wasn't because he'd lacked ties to this world but because he'd pieced things together. That was why he seemed so heartbroken when saying goodbye to Colette. He'd realized his own daughter had killed him and accepted the bittersweet truth: he'd ultimately been the architect of his own downfall.

Tears streamed down Colette's face. "It does not matter. He is the reason my mother died alone and in pain. He deserved what he got, and I was right to do it." She raised the knife and took a step closer.

Grace jumped in front of her daughter, arms spread wide. "Please, no more killing. It hurts my heart. I didn't want this for you, for your sweet soul. I only ever wanted what was best for you."

"Stop, Colette." I held out my hand and winced as my injury flared. "Grace wouldn't want this."

She gripped the knife even harder, knuckles turning white. "Do not speak of her. You did not even know her."

"Not in life, but her spirit is with us now. I can speak to her through this." I pulled out the chain from under my shirt and showed her the charm.

Her eyes widened, but she didn't move. "I thought I lost it the night of the fire. That was my mother's. I sent it to her when I was a child to remind her of me. Give it back!"

"She wants you to stop." I tried to control the tremor in my voice. "This is not why she sacrificed for you, why she broke her own heart so you would have a better life, one far away from her family's judgment, from Roman's influence. She wouldn't want you to throw your life away by exacting revenge on her behalf. Stop before you make it any worse."

My focus flicked to Nolan. I'd been as blind as Colette. "Someone once made a great sacrifice for me, and it wasn't because he expected something in return. He wanted me to be happy. And that's all your mother wants for you. By continuing to hurt and kill in her name, you're spitting on everything she wished for you. So please, for your mother, drop the knife."

Colette's shoulders shook as she succumbed to sobs. The blade dropped from her hand and clattered to the floor. She fell to her knees, hunching over and giving in to her grief.

Grace went to her side to comfort her. But once she'd wrapped her arms around her daughter, she glowed brighter and brighter until I could barely look at the pair. Finally, in a burst of warm light, she vanished, leaving behind sparks that showered down on Colette.

It wasn't the happy ending I'd wished for the ghost, forced to watch her daughter do so much harm to both others and herself. However, perhaps she'd found comfort in knowing the drama was over and there was nothing more to do for her child. Her job as a mother had come to an end, and she could move on. I just hoped it was to rest in peace.

Bang. The front door burst open.

The sheriff stepped into the home, his stout frame backlit by the setting sun. Gun extended, he trained it on the sobbing figure. When Colette stared up at him with red, puffy eyes, she held out her wrists to be cuffed.

His sharp gaze surveyed the room, settling on me and then my arm. "Anyone else in here?"

I blinked, momentarily stunned by his sudden entrance. "N-No. It's only the two of us."

With a nod, he holstered the gun and pulled out a set of cuffs. He bent down in front of Colette and fastened them on her. Relaxing slightly, I glanced at my throbbing, bloody arm and noticed I was still clutching the urn. Gently, I set it down.

Making sure Reed was distracted, I slipped off my necklace and placed the Eiffel Tower charm next to the remains. I didn't care if they found it, so long as they didn't find it on me.

"I'm sorry," I whispered to Grace, unsure if she could hear me anymore.

Heavy boots thudded up the front steps a second before Jason barreled in. He scanned the scene before rushing to my side. "Are you okay?"

"I think so," I said, a little surprised by the fact. "How did you know I was here?"

"We got an anonymous phone call from someone in the area about ten minutes ago."

I thought back to my quiet walk there. Who would have seen me? There were no houses nearby, and the last time I checked, hawks didn't have cell phones.

The thought of the bird gave my brain a jolt, and I raced across the house to where Colette had trapped it. However, when I found the laundry basket, it was lying on its side, empty.

I whirled around, searching for the injured bird, but there was no sign of it.

Nolan pointed to the back of the house. "Vi, look."

I turned to find the back door ajar. It had definitely been locked before.

Adrenaline, shock, or pain must have been playing mind games with me—likely all the above. Logically, I knew a bird couldn't have opened the door. Yet when I searched the backyard, already deep in shadow from the fading twilight, there wasn't so much as a flutter of feathers.

A siren wailed nearby, growing closer. Over it, I heard a cry pierce the air above me. I raised my gaze skyward and spotted a great hawk circling overhead, a little unsteadily. It made one more loop above me, wings fluttering out of sync, before it glided off into the distance.

"Thank you," I whispered before the bird disappeared from sight.

CHAPTER TWENTY-FOUR

In the end, the cut on my arm wasn't so bad. It took only ten stitches, a bandage, and some choice words muttered under my breath throughout the process. The nurse was putting the finishing touches on the dressing when the closed privacy curtain shifted and two sets of boots appeared beneath it.

"You're good to go," the nurse told me. "When you're ready, stop by the desk to sign some forms."

Once she'd gathered her supplies, she swished the curtain aside and slipped out. It didn't close all the way behind her, so Sheriff Reed and Deputy Swan took this as an invitation to come in. They must have been there with more questions. I would have preferred more stitches. Feeling like I was already at a disadvantage, I swung my legs over the side of the bed and sat taller so I was looking straight into the sheriff's eyes.

He gestured to my bandaged arm. "Glad to see you're okay."

I knew he didn't care about my well-being, so I stared blankly at him. "What can I help you with?"

"There are a few gaps I need you to fill in. Not too many, though. Colette was thorough when she confessed." He frowned and ran a thumb over his mustache. "Actually, it was a little too easy."

"Isn't that a good thing? For the investigation, I mean," I quickly clarified since the magic cinnamon roll still coursed through my system. Truthfully, it wasn't a good thing for Colette.

Guilt nagged at me over how I'd taken away her free will. Well, her free will to come clean anyway. Deciding to go stabby stabby with the dessert knife was on her. While bringing her to justice felt right, how I'd gone about it felt less so. That was on me.

Helen's words came back to me. *There are no good or bad powers, but witches are defined by what we do.*

"Usually, it's a good thing," the sheriff relented. "This time, though, it was… strange."

I bit my lower lip before I could blurt, "Or magical."

When I said nothing, Reed's eyes narrowed. "How did you know Colette was behind the attacks?"

Oh, boy. Was that a loaded question or what? Any other time, I would have rubbed how I'd solved it in his face. Unfortunately, I had to focus on constructing a story full of partial truths. "I didn't know at first. I discovered Roman and Grace had a child, so they were high on my list of suspects. But it wasn't until I went to check out Grace's old house and found Colette living there that the pieces fell into place."

His eyes narrowed even further until it was a wonder he could see me. "So you just popped by with some baked goods and asked her if she killed Roman?"

"Yep, pretty much," I said then clamped my lips tight.

My breaths grew labored from the effort of holding back so much of the story. Like how I'd enlisted a cat to steal evidence, asked for a ghost's help, magicked a confession out of Colette, and suspected a hawk was stalking me.

When my tongue moved of its own accord, I chomped down on it and groaned. As a cover for my strange behavior, I touched my bandage gingerly, pretending pain was the cause. It still wasn't a lie because it did smart.

Thankfully, Reed let it go and consulted his notes. "Colette said something odd during her confession. Apparently, you told her you're a witch."

Perfect.

I'd deleted the recording of our visit from my phone, hoping that, by some miracle, she'd keep that far-fetched tidbit to herself. But deep down, I'd known it was too much to ask. And now, the spell was urging me to confirm it.

Lie, lie, lie, I begged my brain. I couldn't. So I chuckled like he must have been joking. "Totally. I'm a witch. Isn't that wild?"

He didn't seem amused. "Why did you tell her that?"

Because it's true. I tried to shove the thought aside, but the admission was there on the tip of my tongue. As I opened my mouth, Jason cut me off.

"Isn't it obvious?" he asked. "She was in danger, so she said something that would disarm her attacker."

Reed kept his cold blue gaze on me. "Why a witch? Why not say 'I've got backup on the way' or anything even remotely believable?"

I was tired of the questions, of his constant suspicion, however warranted it was. I'd wrapped up his case and tied it with a neat little bow for him. What more did he want?

"Would you mess with a witch, Sheriff Reed?" I asked. "Wouldn't you be afraid that I'd curse you or turn you into a toad or something?" I wiggled my fingers in a silly "abracadabra" gesture.

Was it my imagination, or did he flinch?

His Adam's apple bobbed. "Still. Strange you'd choose a witch. Why not a vampire?"

"It was daytime," I shot back.

"A demon?"

"My complexion is too clear, and I have a distinct lack of horns."

I figured he must have been messing with me. Or else this was a strange interrogation tactic. Then I recalled the night he'd been lurking outside Helen's house. The night I'd learned about my powers. I didn't know how much he'd overheard, but the way he was pushing the subject now made me certain the answer was "too much."

Reed stepped closer. "You being a witch would actually make sense. I mean, I still can't explain how you got to shore the night of the car accident."

"Me neither," I said, which was the truth. "But it's not because I'm a mermaid."

He sniggered but not at my joke. More in the way a cat might jeer at a mouse trying to fight back.

Helen had been right to warn me against using the magic cinnamon rolls. At the time, all I'd thought about was Alice's freedom—what could be more important than that? Now, it was obvious I'd been rash. Through Colette's confession, had I given a name to Reed's suspicions about me? Or, worse, put Helen and Alice at risk too?

When the heavy silence dragged on, Jason cleared his throat. "As helpful to the case as this conversation is, I think Alice is here to pick up Vi."

I jumped off the bed, eager to see her. "You already released her?"

"Of course." The sheriff tilted his chin as if offended I even had to ask. "She did nothing wrong."

"I know," I said, both because I was a slave to the truth and I felt smug.

"At least Caitlin's family finally has answers. Hopefully, it will provide some comfort to know her killer is headed to prison."

While I hoped so, too, I didn't think anything could ease their grief at a time like this.

He placed his hat on his head and tipped it. The brief pause at the end made me wonder if it was a subtle acknowledgment that I'd solved another case for him. Only one more to go: Nolan's.

"I'll contact you if I have any more questions." He shoved the curtain aside and strolled out.

I hoped he meant questions about the case and not witchcraft.

Jason lingered behind. Now that the official part of his visit was over, he pulled me in for a hug. "Thank you. I don't know how you did it, but thank you."

After a moment, I gave him a pat on the back, and he followed the sheriff out. I waited a few minutes to ensure they'd both left the building then signed myself out at the nurse's station and exited the treatment area. When I reached the hall, Nolan was there, hands in his pockets, the toe of his dress shoe tapping. I didn't want to dwell on how it made an actual noise—one that I could hear anyway.

At the sight of me, his rigid posture melted. "There you are. How are you feeling?"

Even though we were alone, I kept my voice hushed. "Not bad, considering. I didn't realize you were here."

"I thought it was best to stay out in case they were doing tests or something. As a ghost, it's easy to cross lines, as you've seen." He rubbed the back of his neck, and I knew he was referring to his sleepover. "Can't tell you how many times I've walked in on someone changing, or worse," he joked.

"I appreciate the space." However, I still needed more. To be under a truth spell while in the company of my dead fiancé was a recipe for disaster. There were a lot of things scrambling to jump out of my mouth. Things I wasn't ready to be candid about.

Pressing my lips tight, I beelined it for the waiting room, where I found Alice. She sat in the chair next to poor Mr. Curry's ghost, unwittingly keeping him company. When she saw me, she leaped to her feet and flew across the room. Nolan stepped aside as she embraced me.

"I'm so glad you're okay," she said.

A tension that had been building inside of me released, and I laughed. "I'm glad you're not in jail."

She squeezed me harder. "All thanks to you. Though if Zelda is to be believed, she's the real hero."

I knew Alice was trying to lighten the mood, but I drew away to look her in the eye. "You don't need to thank me for fixing the problem I created. None of this would have happened if I hadn't pushed you so hard to open your business. You wouldn't have even been at the engagement party if it hadn't been for my meddling."

Her forehead creased. "That's not true."

"Actually, it is. I couldn't lie to you even if I tried." After a glance around, I lowered my voice. "I ate one of your cinnamon rolls at Colette's."

Her eyes grew round. "You're kidding me."

"There's a lot more we should talk about. But I want you to know, after watching you in the kitchen over the last couple of days, I realized you don't need me butting into your business— baking or otherwise. You're going to do amazing things."

She straightened, delicate chin rising. "You're right. I am. This entire ordeal has shown me I can handle more than I thought. I'm pretty sure prison has changed me."

I choked out a surprised snort. "You only spent a few hours in the sheriff's holding cell."

"I'm considering getting a tattoo that says 'Bad Batch.' You know, because I'm bad to the bone now."

We broke into a fit of giggles and headed for the exit, where I glimpsed Helen's car parked outside. Alice must have borrowed it to pick me up. While we were a quick fifteen-minute walk from home, I was grateful. My face-off with Colette had depleted my energy.

The automatic doors hissed open at our approach. Alice

continued to walk through, but Nolan and I automatically stepped out of the way as an older woman entered. It wasn't until Alice gave me a strange look that I discovered she couldn't see her. I did a double take. It was Milton's mother.

Mrs. Curry gave me a nod before she anxiously scanned the waiting room's empty seats. At least, to anyone else, they would appear empty. When she spotted the semitransparent figure rocking and moaning in pain, she gasped and brought a shaking hand to her mouth.

Alice eyed me warily, like she thought I should stay overnight for observation. "Are you coming?"

"In a second."

Although I couldn't tear my attention away from the reunion, I felt Nolan beside me, watching with quiet intensity. He hardly moved, like he'd forgotten how to take a ghostly breath.

As Mrs. Curry shuffled toward her late husband, something about her changed. Her expression softened, filling with the love of a youthful woman until she almost looked like the man's young bride again. I rubbed my eyes and discovered it wasn't my imagination.

Her white hair darkened, and the wrinkles melted from her face as she transformed into the woman I recognized from the old wedding photo. Back straightening, her shuffle lengthened until she was by his side in two more strides.

The cannery worker took in her familiar face. His features, which were creased from years of pain, relaxed, giving way to a brilliant smile. The hole in his chest closed in on itself, as if being with her made him complete, and he stood to embrace her.

While they didn't exchange words, they seemed to come to a decision. Hand in hand, the newlywed couple strolled through the doors and into the night. After losing so many years, I hoped they'd finally get the time together they deserved. But they'd hardly taken a few steps before their figures dissolved into smoke. Twisting in the wind, they drifted away to whatever came next.

I slid my gaze to Nolan, who hadn't moved through the entire scene. He stared, transfixed, at the spot they'd disappeared, longing etched on his face. No. Jealousy.

Automatically, I reached out to him until I remembered myself. "Your time will come."

"When?" He turned his tortured expression on me. "I can't wait over fifty years like they did."

"I helped them. I'll help you too."

I just wished I knew how.

CHAPTER TWENTY-FIVE

Spring was in the air. It was still early in the season, but as I strolled to work, I soaked in the energy: early-bird tourists, flower baskets spilling with new blooms, and sale signs that encouraged out with the old, in with the new. A chance for a do-over. I certainly needed one of those.

Part way down Beluga Boulevard, I stopped by the charred remains of Spread the Word and was met with a beautiful sight. A collection of blossoms, everything from expensive bouquets to wild flowers, consumed the boardwalk in front of the shop.

Notes and cards expressing love for Caitlin dotted the arrangement, many of which were postcards from around the world. They displayed some of the most popular destinations and picturesque sites. While her ghost hadn't stuck around for long, part of me hoped she might somehow still get to travel to all the places she'd dreamed of visiting.

I knelt before the tribute and set down a small bouquet of early blooms I'd picked from my backyard. Okay, I'd also snuck a couple of nicer flowers from Helen's garden. I pulled out a postcard from my pocket, one I'd sent Dad from Santorini, Greece. He'd kept it on the fridge all this time, but when I asked if I could take it, he said he didn't mind. The island had been one of the most relaxing places I'd spent time in, and after the violence that had taken Caitlin, I liked to imagine her there.

After nestling the postcard into the flowers, I continued down the boardwalk. As I passed Full of Beans, I nearly ran into a couple coming out with to-go cups. When I saw who it was, a smile stretched across my face. Heads bent close, Pepper Moon and Milton Curry hardly seemed aware of their surroundings or anything that wasn't each other.

As we crossed paths, they finally noticed me, and each gave me a knowing look. I grinned back, a happy thrill running through me at the matchmaking success, and carried on.

Despite the early hour, the promenade was already buzzing with visitors taking in the fresh air and scenic views. Joining them, I leaned against the railing. It was easy to live in such a beautiful place and forget to stop and smell the sea air sometimes. Tourists reminded me how lucky I was to live on Charm Island.

My phone dinged with a text, and I drew it out of my pocket.

ALICE

I got it! I got the contract for the resort.

Squealing, I hugged my phone. Fireworks of joy burst inside me, and I quickly texted back.

That's amazing. We'll celebrate tonight at the Clam Shell. My treat.

Basking in the joyful news, I took a moment to scan the marina. I half expected to see my stalker hawk overhead, keeping an eye on me. However, I was surprised to discover the *Crescent* floating in its usual spot, with Max's muscular figure moving about the deck. As though he sensed me staring, he glanced my way.

Even from this distance, I worried he'd notice my blush. I waved, and he raised his hand in return. Only then did I notice his left arm was in a sling.

It might have been because my hawk friend had just crossed my mind, but a strange thought hit me. Max's injury was to the same arm—er… wing—that the bird had injured. I quickly dismissed the musing. Because it was silly… right?

Max resumed his chores, and I hurried into Charming Treasures, a little more distracted now. My focus kept returning to that hawk and how, without its interference in Colette's home, I probably wouldn't be alive. Then, there was that strange sea creature that had assisted me in the marina with the last murderer I'd taken down. While I hadn't seen what had saved me, there were endless tales of dolphins helping humans. Were the island's animals suddenly interested in solving crimes? Or was there something larger at work?

Even once Dad left the shop to take his break, I couldn't concentrate. I picked away at mindless tasks, tidying and rearranging displays. Finally, the bell above the door chimed. Grateful for the distraction, I spun to face the customer and found Kinsley's effervescent smile on the other side of the counter.

"Hi," I greeted her. "How have you been, you know, after what happened at the party?"

She pulled a face. "It was disappointing, but we're doing okay. It was all that Colette woman's fault. Roman's, too, I suppose."

After the terrible unfolding of events, the truth had come out about Roman, Grace, and their daughter. Honestly, I was amazed that piece of gossip had remained hidden for so long. In the end, the town attributed the partygoers' wild behavior to side effects from the poisoned cake. Of course, Colette hadn't poisoned the whole thing, but it was the most logical explanation and therefore the one adopted by the rumor mill. Obviously, Kinsley believed it, too, and I wasn't going to correct her.

"I'm just sorry Alice got wrapped up in all of it," Kinsley said. "I hope she doesn't regret doing the party."

"She was thrilled to have the opportunity," I told her. "And she's doing pretty well for herself now. Since Spread the Word is gone, all the coffee shops and corner stores are banging on her door to fill their baking needs. Plus, she just got the contract to bake for the new resort once it's open."

"I'm so happy for her. No one is more deserving. After the beautiful job she did, I'm going to hire her to bake my wedding cake. I don't care what my parents say." She winced. "By the way, I heard what my mom said to you. I'm so sorry. You know I don't feel the same way, right? While I'm sad my brother isn't here, I'm glad you are."

To hear those words coming from Nolan's sister hit me harder than it could have from anyone else, maybe even Nolan himself. For that gift, I rounded the counter and dragged her into a hug.

I wanted to say her brother was still around, watching over her, and how happy he was about the upcoming wedding. But something stopped me. For one, I didn't want it getting back to her father that I had powers. It was already bad enough that Sheriff Reed's radar was in overdrive. More importantly, I suspected she was better off not knowing. She'd found peace, and I didn't want to disturb that. The knowledge of Nolan's restless spirit was mine to bear.

When we pulled apart, I asked, "What brings you in today?"

She heaved a dramatic sigh. "We've been so busy with wedding planning that we haven't even ordered our rings yet." She took my hands in hers. "I wouldn't want anyone but you to make my wedding band."

Joy and affection for the young woman welled inside me. "I would be honored."

As she browsed through our limited selection of rings, I pulled out some idea books I'd put together. They contained examples of work I'd done in the past and 3D renderings of bolder ideas I hadn't tried yet. I spread them on the counter, turning them to face her.

"Just flag the ones you're interested in." I handed her a stack of sticky notes.

Her face lit up like a kid at Christmas, and she began flipping pages. I busied myself cleaning the counters to give her space, but then something she'd mentioned sank in. If she knew what her mother had said to me, that meant she'd been aware of Nolan's powers. Perhaps she even had some of her own.

"So, are you like your brother?" I asked. "Are you…?"

"Magical?" she asked as if this were a completely normal conversation. "I wasn't sure if you knew about that."

I smiled but didn't explain that this was a recent revelation.

"No. I take after my mom. Dad and Nolan were the magical ones." She flipped to the next page and placed a sticky note on top of it. "It was like they were part of a club, and Mom and I weren't invited. Dad always treated him differently. I know he loves me, but Nolan was the chosen one." She rolled her eyes.

So my suspicions about the mayor had been right. He had powers. While I was desperate to discover what those were, it was more important to find out what Kinsley knew about the accident.

"Everything about that night still weighs on me," I said. "One thing I don't understand is why your father didn't push for the investigation to continue. It was as though he wanted it to go away."

She gave me a cheeky "duh" look. "Of course he did. He's not just the mayor of the town. He's a leader for all magical people on this island and needs to protect them. If the sheriff kept digging into your unbelievable survival, it might have exposed the entire magical community. So Dad made it go away. Besides, he believes it was an accident. It was an old car after all."

Kinsley seemed sad but resolute. I wished I felt the same.

The news her dad was some kind of magical figurehead was a shock, but did he really think it was an accident, or had he told his daughter that to protect his princess from the truth? I didn't want to upset her by suggesting otherwise, so I said, "Nolan loved that car."

Her gaze grew distant. "I just wish the malfunction had been caught at the shop earlier that day. Everything would have been so different." She sighed and closed the idea book. "Do you mind if I take these home with me overnight?"

"That's fine." I gathered them up for her, but I was still mulling over what she'd said. "Wait. You mean someone had worked on the car earlier that day?"

"That's right. He took it into Wheels and Reels." She lifted the stack of books off the counter. "Thanks for the help. I'll stop by again tomorrow with some thoughts."

I rushed to open the door for her and waved goodbye as she headed across the promenade. While I watched her leave, I thought back to those days, to the auto-body-slash-boat-repair place in town. Or, rather, to who'd worked there at the time.

There was only ever one person Nolan allowed beneath the hood of his baby. Which meant the last person with access to the car before it lost control and drove off the cliff was the man who he'd been fighting with.

Max.

～

THANKS FOR READING

I hope you enjoyed reading *Third Crime's the Charm*. If you have a moment, I would be so grateful if you would leave an honest review online. Reviews are crucial for any author, and even just a sentence or two can make a huge difference. I genuinely appreciate your time and support.

Thanks!
Casey

ACKNOWLEDGMENTS

Thank you to my husband and daughter, who haven't banished me yet despite all the stories and characters that possess me. As always, it's been a real scream working with Claire Taylor and Becca Syme to vanquish my writing demons, of which there are many sometimes.

To my editors, Dayna M. Reidenouer, Jennifer Herrington, and Kimberly Husband, your ability to find the errors haunting my books is downright scary. And I couldn't have brought this story to life without my beta readers: Claire Merle, Veronica McIntyre, and Kathy Brenzi. Without all of you, writing would be a curse.

ABOUT THE AUTHOR

Casey Griffin spent her childhood dreaming up elaborate worlds and characters. Now, she writes those stories down. As a jack-of-all-trades, her résumé includes registered nurse, heavy equipment operator, English teacher, photographer, and pizza delivery driver. She's a world traveler and has a passion for anything geeky. With a wide variety of life experiences to draw from, she loves to write stories that transport readers and make them smile. Casey lives in Southern Alberta with her family, and when she's not traveling, attending comic conventions, or watching *Star Wars*, she's writing every moment she can.

CASEYGRIFFIN.COM